The Princess School

Thorn in Her Side

The Princess School

If the Shoe Fits

Who's the Fairest?

Let Down Your Hair

Beauty Is a Beast

Princess Charming

Apple-y Ever After

Thorn in Her Side

and coming soon . . .

Slippery Steps

The Princess School

Thorn in Her Side

Jane B. Mason ᷒ Sarah Hines Stephens

SCHOLASTIC INC.

New York Toronto London Auckland Sydney
Mexico City New Delhi Hong Kong Buenos Aires

Copyright © 2006 by Jane B. Mason and Sarah Hines Stephens.

All rights reserved.
Published by Scholastic Inc.
SCHOLASTIC and associated logos are trademarks
and/or registered trademarks of Scholastic Inc.

ISBN 0-439-79873-6

12 11 10 9 8 7 6 5 4 3 2 1   6 7 8 9 10 11/0

Printed in the U.S.A.   40

First printing, January 2006

For Emily and Madeleine, who are always there to help remove the thorns.

—JBM & SHS

The Princess School

Thorn in Her Side

Chapter One
Come to Play

Briar Rose stamped her dainty feet on the cobbled bridge in front of Princess School. Behind her, the ornate castle looked as though it was decorated for a holiday. The spires were hung with long tapering icicles, the rooftops were covered in white snow, and the windows were etched with delicate frosty patterns. The entire school glittered in the low winter sun. Rose could have gazed at it for hours...if it weren't so bitterly cold.

Rose wrapped her fur-lined cloak more tightly around her. She stamped her feet again, both from cold and impatience. Where were her friends? She couldn't wait to tell them her news.

Rose was about to give up and wait for her friends inside when she spotted something colorful coming out of the gray winter woods. The cold wind stung her eyes and made them water, but even with blurred vision Rose recognized the light step of the emerging figure. Only Snow White could skip on an icy path!

"What are you doing out here in the cold?" Snow smiled as she slid to a halt beside Rose.

Rose blinked, trying to adjust her eyes to the riot of color that encircled Snow. She appeared to be wearing—

"Isn't it lovely?" Snow asked, not minding at all that Rose was staring. "The dwarves sewed all of their old quilts together to make it for me! They didn't want me to catch a chill." She looked down to admire the creation.

Rose smiled back at Snow and her cloak of seven bright quilts. "It's certainly unique!" Snow's clothes were always a little odd, but somehow the pale princess pulled it off. And the thought of Snow's seven surrogate fathers sacrificing their quilts—even old ones—for Snow's comfort was truly heartwarming.

While Snow and Rose admired the patchwork wrap, their friend Rapunzel sneaked up behind them. Her abundant auburn hair was wrapped around her head and neck like a hat and muffler. Tiny jewel-like crystals of ice had formed all over the coils of braid.

"Rapunzel! How clever of you to use your hair to keep warm!" Snow exclaimed.

"Mmmf," Rapunzel mumbled through her hair. She started herding her friends toward the warmth of the castle.

"Wait, there's Ella!" Rose waved as Cinderella Brown dashed down the lane toward them. She was picking her feet up like a cat in a puddle, trying to keep them from touching the ground for too long. Ella was wearing the same thin slippers Snow had gotten for her at the beginning of the school year—slippers meant for dancing, not walking through snow. Her feet must have been freezing! Rose made a mental note to bring her some boots. Ella's horrible stepmother never bought Ella anything new, but Rose's own closets were overflowing.

"So!" Rose let out her breath as the door to Princess School whooshed shut behind the four friends. They stood together in the warmth and splendor of the grand entry hall. "You simply cannot guess what I saw on the way to school today!"

"A rabbit?" Snow guessed.

"A dragon?" Rapunzel spat a long hair out of her mouth.

"A blooming bulb?" Ella shivered.

"No, no." Rose shook her head. "The Calliope Players! My coach passed their caravan on the way here."

3

Snow clapped her mittened hands with excitement. "The Calliope Players!" she exclaimed. "Do you think they were on their way to Princess School?"

"They might be," Rose replied. "Remember, the headmistress said we would have some surprise guest instructors for the short winter term."

The winter term was special. For two weeks, none of the aspiring princesses attended regular classes. Instead, they prepared a grand play to celebrate the winter season. All of the Princess School students would work together on the production. Rose knew her friends were as excited as she was to get started.

"I wonder what the play will be? I can't wait for the auditions!" Rose simply adored playacting. She enjoyed the freedom of being someone—anyone—other than herself, even if it was just for pretend. In real life, Rose was an only child, and her overprotective parents often drove her crazy. Her father was so concerned about Rose's safety, he had wanted her to wear gauntlets on the first day of school! And her seven guardian fairies were so fretful about everything that Rose was barely allowed to do anything on her own. It was terribly stifling!

"I think I might like to work on the costumes," Ella said. She was still hopping from foot to foot to warm her toes.

"I don't think I want to act." Snow giggled. "I might blush."

"How about painting sets?" Rose suggested. "You do have a way with color."

Snow laughed again with delight. "Perfectly perfect!" she exclaimed.

Rose watched Rapunzel quickly unwrap and recoil her unruly hair on the top of her head. As much as Rapunzel complained about Looking Glass class, she had certainly picked up some useful tricks! In no time her ridiculously long tresses were twisted and wrapped neatly in a large bun with several thick braided loops hanging down her back. "I wonder if there will be an orchestra," Rapunzel mused.

"Do you play?" Ella's eyes lit up. She loved music.

"Well, no," Rapunzel admitted.

Rose smiled at her friend. Rapunzel was always up for trying something new. No doubt she could learn to play any instrument there was—though perhaps not during the short winter term.

The warning trumpet sounded and the four girls hurried toward hearthroom. All around them in the halls other students were also discussing the play. Rose caught tiny snippets of their conversations.

"I do hope it's a comedy."

"I hope it's something romantic!"

"I can't wait to try out!"

Rose pulled open the hearthroom door for her friends. She could barely contain her smile as she slipped into the chamber behind them. She loved doing things with all of her friends. *And,* she thought, *I might convince Rapunzel to audition yet.*

Chapter Two
Look Sharp

The girls had barely taken their seats when Madame Garabaldi swooped into the room. She did not pause for fanfare or for the assistance of pages. She strode to the front of the room and looked purposefully at her class full of first-year students, called Bloomers. In their second year at Princess School, the students were called Sashes. Third-years were Robes and fourth-years were Crowns. In spite of the excitement in the air and the absence of regular classes, Madame Garabaldi was business as usual.

"I expect," the teacher said firmly, "that each of you will be on your very best behavior during this special term."

Rose noticed that Madame Garabaldi paused before the word *special*.

"Our schedule may have been thrown to the wolves, but the willy-nilly nature of the term is not an excuse to act like goofuses."

Rose hid a small smile. She had never heard Madame G. use words like *willy-nilly* and *goofuses*. Rose was getting the distinct impression that Madame Garabaldi did not approve of the winter term.

With one last stern look at the young princesses in her hearthroom, Madame Garabaldi waved to the page by the door. He opened it promptly. The instructor waved again as if shooing away bothersome insects. The girls were excused. But where were they supposed to go next?

"The Calliope Players are waiting for you in the royal auditorium," Madame G. said with a resigned sigh. With that, the silence was broken and all of the novice princesses leaped to their feet as regally as possible and hurried out the door and down the long corridor toward the auditorium.

Though none of her friends actually tried to speak over the buzz of the crowd making its way down the hall, Rose knew they were as thrilled as she was. Snow grabbed Rose's hand and squeezed. Rose squeezed back.

The auditorium was enormous and lovely. Giant chandeliers hung from the vaulted ceilings. The velvet seats could hold a crowd of hundreds and still not fill the balcony. But by far the most impressive thing in the large room was the stage. It was huge and slanted slightly toward the house seats. It was hung with a heavy red velvet drape nearly two stories tall, and ringed around the front with softly glowing lanterns.

The girls sat down in the audience just as the head-mistress, Lady Bathilde, strode up the stairs to stand in front of the curtain. She looked much happier about the winter term than Madame Garabaldi had. In fact, she looked positively tickled.

"Welcome to the winter term. It is with great plea-sure I announce the play that we will be putting on this year: *The Tale of the Scary Fairy.*" Lady Bathilde paused and smiled broadly as a rush of excited whis-pers filled the room. "As many of you certainly know, *The Tale of the Scary Fairy* is a unique story with many challenges. I am confident that you royalettes will rise to the occasion beautifully...with the help of our spe-cial guests."

Rose smiled broadly. She had never seen Lady Bathilde so excited. Their lovely headmistress was always poised and regal, never...giddy.

"It gives me the utmost pleasure to present to you the menagerie that will help us with this season's play. They need no introduction, as they are known through-out the land. So without further ado, I give you the Calliope Players!"

Madame Bathilde bowed with a flourish and backed away from center stage. Rose's eyebrows shot up in surprise at the headmistress's gesture. Usually others bowed down before *her*. The Calliope Players must really be something special!

A few of the girls in the audience gasped as pages extinguished the lanterns around the house seats. The students fell silent and the curtain went up.

Suddenly Rose was transported. The Calliope Players put on a quick and wordless show to demonstrate their skill. They danced and leaped. Their bodies spoke volumes. Each of the dozen actors was amazing, but Rose could not take her eyes off of one in particular—a small purple-and-green fairy. Though his body was wrapped in a heavy cloak, his wings beat as quickly as a hummingbird's. When they did slow, Rose noticed that the edges of the gossamer wings were barbed and ended in many tiny points, like a delicate saw. His dark hair looked stiff and bristly. He was covered in cloth from head to foot, including the tiny gloves he wore on his hands. He looked as if he had to protect himself from his own sharp edges!

Even from a distance, Rose could see the strong resemblance he bore to her own pack of fliers. He could be their brother! Except this fairy clearly did not share her fairies' cheerful disposition. Perhaps it was his prickly costume or the part he was playing, but his scowl seemed so deep that Rose imagined a smile might break his tiny face.

Completely captivated by the grouchy fairy, Rose was startled when Rapunzel nudged her elbow. She suddenly realized that the rest of the students in the hall were standing and applauding. The skit was over.

Leaping to her feet, Rose added her clap to the thunderous applause. Just when she thought she could not get any more excited, Lady Bathilde took the stage again and announced that there would be a brief pause for tea, in which the girls could mingle with the players.

"I hope you will introduce yourselves and put your best face forward. You represent Princess School, after all," the headmistress reminded them.

"I want to meet Calliope," Ella whispered as the girls followed the energized throng of princesses through the carved auditorium into the hall. "She must be amazing. She runs her own troupe!"

Rose knew who she wanted to meet—the sharp little fairy. But Rapunzel was most interested in the food. "I hope they have tarts," she said, hurrying toward a table laid with tea and cakes.

The crowd of girls and instructors and thespians milled about. Rose stood on tiptoe to try to catch a glimpse of toothed wings. Craning hard to see over the crowd, Rose lost her balance. She stepped back and put her arm out to catch herself against the wall. At the same instant she heard a buzzing sound in her ear.

"You nearly crushed me," grumbled a low voice. It was the fairy!

"Begging your pardon." Rose bowed her head and curtsied. "I didn't see you there. I am so pleased to make your acquaintance. I am Briar Rose." Rose offered her hand. It hung in the air. The fairy simply hovered, glaring at her.

He must still be mad at me for stumbling into him, Rose thought. Close up he looked even more like her fairies. Could he be a cousin? She was about to ask when he finally spoke again.

"Who?" he demanded, still not taking her offered hand. "Who did you say you were?"

"Briar Rose, if it pleases you." Rose bowed again. She had never been received in so gruff a manner before. She wasn't quite sure what to do.

"Nothing pleases me." The fairy buzzed a bit farther away. His eyes were almost purple and they seemed to spark as he stared at her. Then the fairy turned on her offered hand and disappeared into the crowd.

"What was that all about?" Ella asked, coming up behind Rose and offering her a tea cake.

"I'm not sure," Rose said, taking the cake. Oddly, she was not offended by the fairy's behavior. She knew actors could be eccentric. If she was given the chance to become one of them, maybe she could shrug off pomp and decorum as easily as he just had—at least for the duration of the production.

Suddenly the crowd grew quiet again. Lady Bathilde was standing near the auditorium doors on a small podium, holding up her hand. In it she held the script for *The Tale of the Scary Fairy*. And beside her stood Calliope Callaway herself! Lady Bathilde motioned to the striking woman beside her.

In a voice that was resonant and clear, the famous director made an announcement. "Princess School Players, it is our honor to assist in this joint production," Calliope began. She wore a deep red gown and had long, dark, curly hair. Rose liked her at once. "I hope many of you will audition with us tomorrow right here after the first trumpet blast. If you wish, you may pick up a script and begin practicing immediately. And for those of you who do not wish to try out for a stage role, there are many other ways you can participate! We'll need girls to work on the sets, the costumes, the lights, even the props. I hope that each of you will find a way to take part in the production." She smiled at the novice princesses before her.

Rose's stomach gave a little jump. Tryouts were tomorrow!

Getting to the Good Part

"It's my turn!" Hagatha screeched, reaching over Ella to snatch the already-battered script out of Prunilla's hand.

"No, it's not. It's mine!" Prunilla snatched it back, scratching her sister and tearing the parchment in the process.

Ella sighed, sat back, and let the two squabble. Her stepsisters, Hag and Prune, were equally matched, and Ella was exhausted. She had been practicing lines with them for what felt like hours and hours (and hours). They had insisted she help them read from the moment they got home from school the day before, and first thing this morning, too. Ella knew that if the two of them weren't cast in lead roles, Ella's stepmother would determine that it was Ella's fault. In Kastrid's mind, *everything* was Ella's fault.

Ella had read Prince Gallant's lines and prompted Princess Perfecta's lines so many times she knew them by heart—and she was not even planning to audition! In spite of all the practicing, Hagatha and Prunilla had not gotten what Ella would call "better." *Louder maybe,* Ella thought, hiding a smile behind her hand. Her screeching stepsisters' attempts to portray Princess Perfecta—the pinnacle of poise and loveliness—were actually quite amusing.

Ella bit her lip as Prunilla dove back into character. She screwed up her long, pinched face and fluttered her stubby lashes over her beady eyes. Then she unleashed an earsplitting whine. "Prince Gallant, my love, I will be with you forever," she screeched at the top of her lungs. It was enough to make a real prince flee in terror.

"Forever and a day." Ella spoke the next line as she thought a real prince in love might. Her voice was filled with emotion.

"Ha!" Hagatha nearly gagged on a laugh. "It's a good thing they'll be keeping you backstage!" she spat at Ella. "You could never be an actor."

Her stepsister's insult rolled right off of Ella's back. She was getting quite good at not letting them upset her. Besides, helping Hagatha and Prunilla practice had gotten her a ride to school. Even though her stepsisters traveled to school in Ella's father's coach every day, Ella was usually forced to walk.

With a lurch, the coach came to a halt. Luckily for Ella there was no time for another read-through.

Hagatha ripped the script from Prunilla's hands and dashed awkwardly out of the coach. Prunilla leaped after her, squealing. Ella took a deep breath. Although her stepsisters were third-year Robes at Princess School, you would never know it by their behavior. Gratefully, she accepted the hand of the coachman and stepped lightly out onto the Princess School bridge. She could not remember the last time she had arrived at school feeling so warm. And early!

Ella followed her squawking steps into the palace school. The older girls' velvet-lined trunks, where they kept their cloaks, texts, and scrolls, were down a separate hall from Ella's. Ella was relieved to hear their grating voices fade to nothing. It felt funny to walk past hearthroom toward the auditorium. Ella almost wanted to skip. Whether she was trying out or not, the excitement surrounding the play was infectious.

Once inside the performance hall, Ella spied Rose immediately. She was sitting in the front row, reading her script. Even from across the room Ella could tell Rose was as excited as she was—maybe more so. She looked about ready to fidget!

"Ella, I'm so glad you're here!" Rose got to her feet and grasped Ella's hand. "I've been dying to tell someone."

"What is it?" Ella let Rose pull her into a seat.

"I know what part I want to try out for," Rose

16

whispered. Her lovely face was lit up like a candle. "The Scary Fairy!"

"You want to be the villain?" Ella was surprised, but only for a moment. Of course Rose wanted to play the Scary Fairy. She loved to strike out of her everyday role as a perfect princess. "You'll be a wonderful bad guy. But what will your parents think?" Ella asked.

Rose scowled. She did not like to be coddled by her parents or told what to do. But before she could respond, Rapunzel and Snow arrived and slipped into the seats behind Rose and Ella. Rose smiled at them as Calliope Callaway took the stage.

"Rose wants to try out for the Scary Fairy!" Ella whispered.

"Perfect!" Rapunzel replied.

Calliope pushed an unruly sable curl off her forehead and looked out at the house. "Is everyone ready?" she asked with a sly, red-lipped smile. Though she was dressed plainly enough in a blue-and-light-green gown, Calliope made a dramatic impression through her voice and demeanor. Ella marveled at how comfortably she spoke to the large group of princesses and strode around the stage.

When no one answered, Calliope tapped the rolled-up script in her palm. "Then let us begin! I would like to start with the roles of Queen Comely and King DoGood. May I have volunteers?"

Several princesses raised their hands and Calliope asked them to take the stage and read in turn. One by one, prospective players tried on the parts.

"Oh, my, aren't they wonderful to watch?" Ella heard Snow whisper to Rapunzel.

Beside her, Rose looked riveted. Her head was still, eyes fixed. But her feet told a different story. Ella watched her toe tapping, once...twice...three times. Rose was anxious. Ella wondered how long her friend would have to wait to read for the Scary Fairy.

Quite a while. After Queen Comely and King DoGood, Calliope asked for girls to read the parts of Hem and Haw, the royal advisors. And after that she asked for volunteers to read the narrator's lines.

The auditions were taking a long time. When a haughty Bloomer took the stage and began telling Calliope how she always put on wonderful plays at home, Ella leaned over and whispered in Rose's ear, "It will be your turn soon."

Rose smiled gratefully. "Is it so obvious I can't wait?" She shrugged a little sheepishly. "I do like watching the tryouts. Wasn't Red wonderful as the narrator?"

Ella nodded. Their fellow first-year Scarlet Hood had done a great job, sweeping her cloak over her shoulder at just the right moment to great dramatic effect.

"Maybe you should read for some of the other roles, too," Rapunzel suggested, leaning forward. "It might be a good way to warm up."

"I suppose that couldn't hurt," Rose agreed. Just then Calliope asked for girls to read for the lead roles—Princess Perfecta and Prince Gallant. Rose raised her hand, just a bit, and Calliope beckoned her to come up.

Ella felt her own heart race as Rose took the stage. When the scene started, Ella caught her breath. Rose was superb. She did not shout like a few of the other girls or speak her lines to the floor. She enunciated clearly and seemed as natural as could be—as at home on the stage as Calliope herself.

Calliope asked Rose to read Princess Perfecta's lines again and again. She kept using new girls to read Prince Gallant's role, but none of them had the presence that Rose had. And, Ella could tell, Rose was holding back. She was waiting to unleash her full performance, waiting for the chance to read for the part she really wanted.

Ella tried to keep her focus on Rose, but to the right of the stage something was creeping farther and farther into her view. Hagatha and Prunilla! They were buzzing at each other, bickering like angry bugs.

"I should read first!" Hagatha whined, quietly but clearly.

"You needn't read at all," Prunilla spat back. She pointed her nose in the air. "As soon as *I* read, the auditions will surely end. I just know I am the perfect Perfecta."

Hagatha reached out and tweaked her sister's cheek, leaving a nasty red mark. "No, I am!" she snarled, forgetting to be quiet. Ella thought her steps were about to start slapping and scratching each other when Calliope clapped her hands.

"Bravo!" The director was chuckling and applauding Hagatha and Prunilla's performance. Ella was startled. She had gotten so wrapped up in watching her stepsisters go after each other she hadn't realized that their antics had caught *everyone's* attention. Calliope, along with the rest of the crowd in the auditorium, had been watching the argument grow and holding back laughter at the ridiculous duel.

Prunilla at least had the sense to blush when she realized they had been fighting to an audience. Her face was almost magenta.

Hagatha tripped over her own tongue, turned her head to cough in Prunilla's face, and finally managed to choke out a sentence. "Is it our turn? Are we on?"

"You have already put on quite a performance," Calliope said.

"Did I get the part? Am I Perfecta?" Prunilla asked, mopping her face on her sleeve.

"No, stupid, I did! *I'm* Perfecta." Hagatha stepped purposefully on her sister's toes, nearly tripping and falling off the edge of the stage.

Calliope held up one hand for mercy. She was laughing so hard, Ella wondered if she could breathe. "Stop," she gasped. "Please. You are both perfect. I have something very special in mind for the two of you."

Ella could barely believe her ears. Calliope was going to allow Hagatha and Prunilla onstage? They were terrible! She turned to give Snow and Rapunzel a look of disbelief. They looked as baffled as she felt. Onstage Rose shrugged her surprise. *Could Kastrid have pulled strings?* Ella wondered. Ella would not put it past her stepmother—she was always fixing things for her awful daughters. But Calliope didn't seem like the kind of person who would run in Kastrid's circles, or put up with her shenanigans.

Having recovered her breath, the director called over a page and spoke softly to him. She looked at Hagatha and Prunilla once more, smiling widely. "I am having two new parts written just for you," Calliope said. "Parts that will be perfect for your unbridled talent."

Hearing that, Ella nearly choked. Rapunzel had to lean forward and knock her on the back twice.

"Great," Rapunzel said, slumping back in her seat. "Auditions aren't even over and our play is already ruined!"

Chapter Four

Part and Parcel

Rapunzel climbed easily over a row of seats to slip down beside Ella. A few nearby girls looked up with dismay. Princesses-in-training didn't generally jump seats, but Rapunzel didn't care. It was the fastest way to her friend—and Ella looked like she needed a pal. The poor girl was in shock! Rapunzel squeezed her hand, but Ella continued to stare at the director in disbelief.

"Goodness, I never would have thought your stepsisters would be called talented!" Snow whispered as she joined them in the front row. She'd taken a route less direct than Rapunzel's—and a bit more ladylike.

"What could Calliope possibly—" Ella didn't finish. Calliope, who had been making notes on a scroll, was calling them back to order.

"I've made a few decisions," she announced. "The part of the narrator will be played by Scarlet Hood."

There was a smattering of applause. Rapunzel nodded her approval.

"The part of Queen Comely will be played by Astrid Glimmer," Calliope continued.

Several Crowns sitting with Astrid clapped with delight and turned to congratulate their friend. Rapunzel clapped, too. Astrid had a regal air but was not pampered or prissy like some of the older girls.

The next part cast was King DoGood. It went to Veronique Sage. The roles of Hem and Haw went to Tiffany Bulugia and Genevieve the Goose Girl.

"What about Rose?" Snow whispered. There was worry in her dark eyes. Rapunzel patted her hand.

"Rose didn't want any of those parts. She wants to play—" Ella was cut off again.

"Before I cast the principal roles," Calliope said, "I would like to talk about the other tasks that will need undertaking. For every job onstage there are at least three backstage. We will need everyone's help to make this the best show it can be."

Finally, Rapunzel thought. She could not wait to get a job and get busy.

"We need volunteers to do costumes, set design and painting, props, lighting, makeup, and hair. We will require several stagehands and an assistant for Hugo, our stage manager. Not to mention musicians for the orchestra." Calliope paced the stage, rattling off jobs and pointing to the different areas of the auditorium that volunteers could report to if they were interested in a specific task.

Rapunzel looked at the Calliope Players standing around the room holding signs. The players were going to do the jobs alongside the Princess School students and teach the girls their skills. Rapunzel looked from SETS to PROPS to LIGHTING. She had no idea there were so many jobs to do within a single show. She needed to narrow it down.

The player holding the SET sign looked friendly. And Rapunzel was good with tools. She began making her way toward her. Snow skipped past, anxious to get her hands in some paint. Ella was already talking animatedly with the man in charge of costumes.

On stage, the princesses who had been cast stood in a cluster along with Rose and a few other hopefuls. "What I need now is a prince," Rapunzel heard Calliope announce thoughtfully. Then Calliope raised her voice excitedly, as if she had just remembered something. "Where is Rapunzel Arugula? Rapunzel, Rapunzel, where are you, my dear?"

Rapunzel looked up, startled, when she heard her name. *Did she say "prince"?*

Rapunzel walked slowly toward the stage and Calliope. The director smiled warmly at her.

"I hear you played the prince's role to great acclaim when you entered—and won!—the Charm School jousting tournament. You are just what I need!" Calliope beamed and pushed Rapunzel next to Rose. Rapunzel was two inches taller—not including her piled-up hair. "Perfect." Before Rapunzel could say a word, Calliope thrusted a script into her hands. "You shall be our Prince Gallant. And you"—Calliope placed a hand on Rose's shoulder—"shall be Princess Perfecta."

Rapunzel opened her mouth to protest, but Rose beat her to it. "But I don't want to play the perfect princess," Rose started to say. Rapunzel watched Rose catch herself and draw a breath. Not wanting to sound ungrateful, she tried again. "Have you already chosen someone to play the Scary Fairy?"

"Of course! How could I forget?" Calliope looked at Rose gratefully. Rapunzel thought she saw a flicker of hope in Rose's eyes. Then Calliope beckoned someone from offstage.

"The part of the Scary Fairy will be played by our own fairy thespian, Nettle!" Calliope beamed.

The prickly little fairy they had seen the previous day flitted onto the stage to hover in the lineup. He was scowling just as he had yesterday, and even Rapunzel had to admit he was pretty intimidating for someone the size of a mouse. He was a good choice—and already in character.

"The rest of the auditionees will play the towns-folk," Calliope declared. "And remember, there are no small parts!"

Rapunzel looked down the line of princesses onstage. The whole cast was assembled. But how on earth had she ended up a part of it?

Chapter Five
Play On

Walking into the auditorium the next morning, Rose felt like she had entered a hive. Everywhere princesses were buzzing about like bees. Girls were onstage painting set pieces, backstage working on costumes, and all around the stage reading lines. It was hard to believe that out of all this chaos a real show would emerge. And in a matter of weeks!

"Oof." Rose was suddenly flattened against the wall as a group of girls swarmed past. It was "the townsfolk." In her flabbergasted state Rose had barely been aware when Calliope had told all of the princesses who had not been cast and had not chosen an offstage task that they would be the townsfolk. Their job was to react to whatever was going on onstage, and they were already rehearsing with the help of one of the players. The dozen or so girls were moving en masse, pausing to "ooh" over a color of paint or "aah" at a possible costume.

At least I'm not one of the townsfolk, Rose comforted herself. Being part of a herd was perhaps the only thing worse than being Perfecta. When Calliope had called Nettle to the stage the day before, Rose's disappointment had felt so large she thought she might choke on it. Today it felt more like a hard knot in her stomach — a knot too tangled to untie quickly.

Making her way to the stage to begin rehearsing, Rose heard a familiar melody. She ducked around a large set piece and found Snow humming and painting. The day was young, but already Snow had tiny spatters of green paint on her pink cheeks and in her ebony hair.

"Oh, Rose, isn't this wooded hillside just lovely?" Snow crooned as she added more paint to the scenery.

Rose agreed. The hills were a riot of grass and flowers — the perfect setting for Snow.

"Perhaps I should add more daisies," Snow said.

A Calliope Player covered in nearly as much paint as the set piece leaned down to look at Snow's work.

"Remember, you are painting a hillside — not a flower garden," he said gently.

"Oops." Snow's cheeks grew a touch more red under the green.

"How about a few trees?" the player suggested.

"With birds and squirrels?" Snow asked. The player

nodded and Snow eagerly got back to work while Rose ducked behind the side curtain.

Backstage, Madame Taffeta, the Stitchery teacher, and a group of princesses were going through a huge trunk of old costumes. Ella was pulling out gown after gown. Each one was more ornate than the next, and Ella's face showed her delight. "Rose, your costume will be so beautiful. Just look at what we have to work with!"

Ella was used to turning her stepsisters' hand-me-down rags into something passable. And Rose had to admit that the rich fabrics and jewels in the Calliope Players' trove were dazzling. There were hats and more hats. Flowing robes, embroidered capes, all manner of breeches, and even hairpieces!

Rose knew that with her fine stitching and such a wealth of material, Ella could do wonders.

"This is ripped. Throw it away!" A very prissy princess picked one of the gowns out of the trunk. She held the torn frock between two fingers and wrinkled her nose at it.

Ella examined the garment. "Why, it's just popped a few stitches," she pointed out. "I can fix it in no time."

Rose didn't try to hide her smile. Ella was so resourceful. She could make the best of any situation no matter how challenging.

Rose read a few lines to herself while she walked back

out onto the stage. She looked up from her script and let her gaze linger on the auditorium's gilded silver ceiling and rose-carved columns. She felt her own excitement, which had gone missing after she was cast in the wrong role, grow. It didn't matter what part she had—what mattered was that she was having this great experience with her friends, and they would make it fun.

"Oof." The herd of townsfolk backed into Rose, almost shoving her off the stage. At the last minute one of them grabbed her arm.

"Sorry, Beauty," the townie whispered.

The townsfolk were supposed to be practicing their idle chatter, but the whole pack was gasping and pointing up in the air, past the lanterns and curtains to the catwalk high above the stage. Rose looked up. Someone was walking back and forth on the narrow ledge that was used by the lighting crew, talking to herself and not paying any attention to the gasping crowd below. Rapunzel!

Leave it to Rapunzel to find a secluded spot in the chaos to practice her lines, Rose thought. *She probably doesn't want anyone to hear her until she can do her part flawlessly.*

Rose glanced around in the wings of the stage, looking for the way up to Rapunzel's roost. She didn't see a ladder, but she did see something else. She turned around as quickly as she could, but it was too late. She had been spotted.

"Oh, Beauty!" Hagatha's singsongy tones were off-key. Rose cringed at the awful nickname and turned back toward the awful girl who had addressed her. Prunilla was standing with her sister and they both looked as smug as cats who'd swallowed canaries.

"We do hope you're not feeling too bad about your part," Hagatha purred.

Rose kept a small smile on her face to hide her shock. Had Ella told her stepsisters that Rose wanted the part of the Scary Fairy? No, Ella despised her stepsisters—and she was too good a friend to reveal Rose's secrets.

"It must be so boring to have to play the same old part just the way it's always been written," Prunilla put in.

Rose nodded now, and her smile turned genuine. Hag and Prune had no idea she had wanted to play the villain. They were just trying to make her jealous because they were having special parts written for them. Rose struggled to keep her grin from breaking into a laugh. She could not imagine being jealous of Ella's steps, not even for a moment.

"It is wonderful to be admired, isn't it?" Hagatha sidled up to Rose. When Rose said nothing, she turned back to Prunilla. "Sister, we're muses!"

Thankfully, Rose did not have to think of a response to that. Calliope called her name from the stage and one other name in addition—Nettle. Practice was beginning.

Nettle buzzed onto the stage already acting the part. He looked, if anything, grumpier than he had the day before. Rose smiled at him but the prickly fairy did not even glance at her. Rose looked at the director, concerned. It did not seem like Nettle wanted Rose to be there at all.

Calliope was unfazed. She simply showed them the passage where she wanted them to begin reading and took a seat in the audience to watch.

It was the scene from the beginning of Act 2, where the Scary Fairy warns Princess Perfecta that she must not wed Prince Gallant.

"You will be sorry, I promise you," Nettle spat.

From his first line, Rose's worries about Nettle faded and her curiosity grew. He was fantastic! When he read his lines it was like he actually *was* the evil fairy. It felt like he would truly put a curse on her if he could.

Rose tried her best to let her feelings ring in her voice the way Nettle did, but beside him she felt flat and dull. Still, Rose was exhilarated—her costar wasn't exactly friendly offstage, but Rose could tell she was going to learn a lot from him.

When the last line had been read, the townsfolk, who had been watching all along, began to applaud.

"Bravo, Beauty!"

"Perfecta perfected!" they called out.

Rose allowed herself a small curtsy. She glanced at the director. Calliope was beaming.

"Great job, Perfecta!" She nodded at Rose. Rose waited for Calliope to compliment Nettle, too. He was obviously the better actor. But Calliope said nothing more. She simply picked up her quill to see what was next on the agenda.

"You were wond—" Rose turned to tell Nettle herself what a fine job he'd done, but he had already disappeared into the wings.

Wow, Rose thought. *I can't wait for our next scene! I just know that I can do better. And I might ask Nettle for a few pointers, too.*

Chapter Six
Surely They Jest

Rapunzel spun on her heel and walked back across the catwalk yet again, reading from her script. "My love for you is as strong as the ocean tides," she murmured quietly. "And will endure as long as the sea itself."

Rapunzel smirked. She didn't usually fall for this mushy romance stuff, but she was actually enjoying learning Prince Gallant's lines. He seemed like a really decent guy—and, thanks to her, he would be excellent on a horse as well.

Too bad the horse isn't real, Rapunzel thought, gazing down at the wooden hobbyhorse waiting for her at the side of the stage. One of the props princesses was putting a bridle over his stuffed head so he would be ready to ride.

Rapunzel let her script fall to her side and slowed her pace to watch the scene below—and not just the scene unfolding onstage. Everywhere in the theater princesses were hard at work on the production. Ella had already pieced the king's and queen's costumes together. Snow was painting animals of all shapes and sizes romping through the forest set, and the trees were in bloom with riotous color. Snow herself sported several bright splotches on her face, hands, gown—even in her dark hair.

Onstage, Rose and Nettle were doing their second run-through of the scene where the Scary Fairy tries to scare Princess Perfecta out of wedding Prince Gallant. Rapunzel stopped moving to watch.

"I'm warning you, wedding that prince could be the very worst—and last—mistake you make," the fairy hissed, swooping to hover right in front of Princess Perfecta's face.

"Don't listen to him!" Rapunzel whispered from her perch with a giggle. She was surprised by how engrossed she was in the play and secretly glad that she knew how this adventure would end—happily.

Rapunzel leaned her elbows on the iron catwalk railing. Rose and Nettle were obviously a well-matched pair. Their concocted sparring looked as real as the furious fights Rapunzel used to have with her foster mother, Madame Gothel, when the witch first discovered that she was climbing out of her tower to attend Princess School.

"Prince Gallant is a good and noble knight," Princess Perfecta replied. "And I shall marry him."

Rapunzel felt a tingle of pride. Rose was talking about her! Or her character, at least. And she had to admit that while she initially hadn't wanted to be in the play, she was feeling excited about it now. It would be a challenge and an adventure—and Rapunzel was always up for both.

Rapunzel unfolded the script and got back to her pacing and practicing. She could be called to the stage at any moment and wanted to have her lines memorized! It wasn't going to be easy to match step with Rose and Nettle.

"The evil fairy cannot harm us now," she said softly, reaching the end of the catwalk. After a dozen more turns she was almost at the end of the script and had most of her lines under her the sash. Prince Gallant would be gallant indeed!

"Rapunzel!" a voice called out from the other end of the catwalk. It was Rose. Ella was with her. Rapunzel suddenly realized that the stage below was empty—everyone was taking a break. "You've been up here all morning," Rose said.

"I was beginning to wonder if you'd disappeared," Ella added with a warm smile.

The two friends started across the catwalk toward Rapunzel. Rose looked down and put a hand on her stomach. "Wow, don't you get a little dizzy walking and reading up here?" she asked, her face suddenly pale. "It's so…high," she finished, unable to tear her eyes from the stage below.

"They should have cast you as a bird," Ella added.

"I like high places," Rapunzel answered with a laugh. "I live in a tower, remember? But I'm ready now—let's head down to the stage." Rapunzel took Rose's hand. "Just don't look down," she suggested as she led her to the end of the catwalk. "It makes it worse."

Soon Rose and Rapunzel were padding down the ladder, with Ella clomping down behind them in the thick winter boots Rose had brought her that morning. Most of the princesses left their boots in their trunks and changed into elegant satin slippers, but Ella was so pleased to have a pair she decided to wear them all day.

Just as the girls reached the bottom step Calliope clapped her hands together briskly. Half of her dark curls were pulled back with a silver barrette, leaving the rest to cascade down her slender back. She smiled broadly. "The final script is ready," she crowed. "Where are Hagatha and Prunilla? Where is that pair of comic geniuses?"

Within half a second the two Robes were hurtling across the stage, tripping over each other in an effort to get to the center first.

"I'm sure my part is the newly created leading role," Hagatha cackled.

"Ha!" Prunilla retorted. "The only leading you'll be doing is with the rein to Prince Gallant's horse!"

Hagatha glared at her sister as she skidded to a halt at center stage and turned toward the audience, with a huge smile showing all of her large yellow teeth. Prunilla crashed into her, and all four of their slippered feet slid out from under them, sending them flailing to the floor.

Rapunzel laughed along with everyone else in the auditorium. Served those two scallywags right. They were so awful in the tryouts! She couldn't imagine what kind of talent Calliope had seen in them. Rapunzel was almost as eager as Hag and Prune to hear about the parts that had been created for them.

"Please step right up to the front of the stage and bow your lovely heads," Calliope said, "so that we may adorn them with the proper finishing touches."

Hagatha and Prunilla's faces lit up like greedy pigs about to devour a bucket of slop. They were practically salivating! Rushing forward, they each knelt on one knee and lowered their heads.

"I'll bet my tiara will have more jewels than yours!" Prunilla hissed under her breath.

Hagatha's response was a simple snort.

Rapunzel glanced at Ella, who was shaking her head.

"Now close your eyes," Calliope instructed, taking a large cloth sack from a page who had scampered onto the stage. Rapunzel craned her neck to get a good look. What could possibly be in there?

Calliope opened the sack and retrieved a pair of brightly colored jester hats, complete with bells on the pointed ends.

Next to Rapunzel, Ella gasped in surprise. The rest of the princesses in the auditorium watched in stunned silence.

Calliope stepped forward and placed the hats on the waiting heads. Hagatha let out a little sigh as hers was slipped on. Rapunzel choked back a laugh. She clearly thought she'd just been crowned!

Calliope stepped back. "You may open your eyes now," she told the girls.

Hagatha and Prunilla opened their eyes, looked at each other, and both smiled triumphantly. "I told you there would only be one more princess," Prunilla said haughtily.

"Indeed, sister," Hagatha agreed. "And it is obviously me."

Prunilla guffawed, then suddenly fell silent. At exactly the same moment, each girl reached up and felt the adornment on her own head. Their faces froze with virtually identical looks of horror as they realized they each had on the headpiece of a courtly clown.

"But..." Hagatha huffed.

"I'm supposed to be..." Prunilla puffed.

"Where's my crown?" they sputtered together.

Chapter Seven
Running Lines

"I can't believe Hagatha and Prunilla got cast as jesters! Did you see the looks on their faces when they realized they weren't wearing crowns?" Rose giggled as she led her friends up the path away from Princess School. They'd just finished rehearsal and had decided to walk home together as far as Snow's cottage. Things had been so busy all day they'd hardly had a chance to talk.

Ella pulled her cloak closely around her and smiled broadly. "That moment alone was worth all the time I had to spend preparing them for auditions," she said.

"Well, they obviously weren't prepared for the roles they got," Rapunzel said with a twinkle in her eye. "Watching them get 'crowned' was the best part of the whole day."

Snow nodded. "They really are perfect for the parts," she said sweetly. "The way they always stumble around, bumping into each other, reminds me of the dwarves when they first wake up in the morning."

"Only I'll bet the dwarves are a lot more cheerful—even at dawn," Rapunzel said. "Those two are like a pair of hungry vultures! Do you suppose that playing jesters might give them a sense of humor?"

Ella shook her head. "Don't count on it."

"They're not the only ones who could use a sense of humor," Snow said, stopping in her tracks so fast that Ella nearly bumped into her. "I just don't understand why that strange fairy is always so grumpy."

Rose smiled to herself. Snow was relentlessly cheerful, and she couldn't imagine why anyone would go around in a bad mood.

"Nettle is *supposed* to act grumpy," Rose explained. "That's what his character in the play is like."

"Sure," Snow said, "he's supposed to act terrible onstage. But when I offered to share my persimmon turnover with him at lunch he didn't even reply. He just glared at me with his tiny black eyes, snatched a piece off the end, and buzzed away! He didn't remove those gloves he always wears, or say a word of thanks. Why, even Gruff has better manners than that!" Snow declared. Rose turned back and saw that Snow's eyes looked misty. Were her feelings really so hurt, or was that from the cold?

"I don't know why he's so cranky offstage," Rose

admitted. "I asked my fairies last night if they knew Nettle. It was quite clear from their huffy reaction that they *do* know him and *don't* like him, but they refused to tell me why."

"I can see why they might not be fond of him," Rapunzel said. "But don't fret, Snow. He's like that with everyone. He flew right into me just before we left and didn't apologize. He hit me right on the cheek, and it only just stopped stinging!" She patted a blotchy spot on her lightly freckled cheek.

"You must admit he is a very skilled actor," Ella said thoughtfully.

"Yes!" Rose agreed. Finally they were talking about what really mattered. Nettle was clearly quite talented. "Did you see how he looked at me with such utter hatred toward the end of the first act? The only time I've seen fairy wings beat that fast was when Petunia was fleeing from a hawk that thought she was a meal on wings."

As Rose talked about Nettle, she found herself filled with admiration for her tiny costar. She hoped they would get a chance to talk tomorrow. She'd looked for him at the end of rehearsal, wanting again to tell him how wonderful he was onstage and how honored she was to be working with him. She thought he might even be willing to offer a few acting pointers—Rose knew she could learn a lot from him. But when she'd opened the door to the dressing room, the fairy had buzzed past without acknowledging her at all.

As her fur-lined boots crunched on the snow—they were almost at the turnoff to Snow's cottage—Rose smiled to herself, thinking about Nettle. Surprisingly, she hadn't been offended by the fairy's abrupt departure from the dressing room, or his silence offstage. In fact, she'd found it kind of refreshing. After being admired and fawned over her entire life, this kind of treatment was utterly new and rather...intriguing.

"Why don't you all come over for a mug of cocoa and a slice of warm bread with butter?" Snow offered, interrupting Rose's thoughts.

Ella stamped her feet in the snow. "That sounds perfect, but I have to get home to serve tea and start supper."

"Can't you tell your stepmother you had to stay late working on costumes?" Rapunzel said with a twinkle in her eye. "Hag and Prune won't be able to tell on you. They looked like they couldn't exit fast enough after Calliope spent the entire afternoon working on their new scenes. Since they left first they could never know if you had to stay late or not."

Ella smiled. "Well, I suppose a quick cup of cocoa couldn't hurt...especially if I don't have to make it myself or serve it on a tray!"

The girls tromped through the snowy clearing to

Snow's front door and pushed it open. Inside, the cottage was cozy and warm. The dwarves were expert fire builders and could make a fire last all day with the proper wood.

Snow lit a couple of lanterns and started the kettle.

"Let's run a few lines," Rose suggested. "I think Gallant and Perfecta should get better acquainted since we didn't get to rehearse today." Rose was feeling especially free, walking home on her own rather than being retrieved by her fairies in her father's coach. Her parents and fairies had been quite relaxed lately. And with the unstructured schedule at school she felt like she had more time to herself than ever.

Rapunzel nodded in agreement and pulled her already slightly tattered script out of her bag. She flipped to the first scene between Prince Gallant and Princess Perfecta. It started with Prince Gallant entering the stage on his horse.

Rapunzel grabbed a broom from next to the fireplace and galloped around the tables and chairs with great gusto. She even whinnied a couple of times for effect.

"Alas, I have seen this countryside many times over but have yet to gaze upon the princess of my dreams. Indeed, I am beginning to think there is nary such a maiden for me," she said in a deeply royal voice, without even glancing at her script.

Rose giggled as she settled herself in the dwarves' biggest chair and demurely spread out the skirt of her gown. Rapunzel was terrific!

"Oh, how I wish a handsome prince would gallop into our small town and save me from this provincial existence," she said forlornly, resting her cheek in her hand and gazing away from Rapunzel.

On cue, Rapunzel galloped up to Rose, skidded her broom to a halt, and looked into the princess's blue eyes. "How now, fair maiden? Why so sullen?" She climbed off her horse and "tied" it to the carved side table. "Surely your life must be as splendid as your lovely face."

Rose beamed up at her friend as she recited her next line. For someone who had no interest in being in the play, Rapunzel was doing great. And she had already memorized most of her part!

As soon as Rose and Rapunzel finished their scene, Ella and Snow leaped to their feet, clapping loudly.

"Bravo!" they cried.

Rose turned to Rapunzel and gave her a quick hug. "You're really good!" she complimented. "Quite princely!"

Rapunzel beamed and placed her horse back in its fireside stable. "I have to admit—I can't wait to try it onstage!"

Chapter Eight

A Faraway Land

Snow dropped the paintbrush she was holding into the can of paint next to her and turned to watch the actors onstage. Hugo, the set master, had asked her to finish the castle piece by the end of the day, but it was so hard to focus with rehearsals going on just a few feet away. Why, every time a new scene unfolded Snow felt as if she'd been transported to a magical faraway land.

"We are so fortunate to have finally been blessed with this beautiful daughter," Queen Comely said onstage now.

Her husband, King DoGood, nodded as he gazed into the baby's bassinet. "She is so perfect in every way. We shall call her... Perfecta."

"Perfecta," Snow whispered, her eyes filling with tears. "What a lovely name!" She knew that the "baby" they were admiring was really a green cabbage wrapped in a blanket, but here in the theater everything seemed possible. She could just imagine the teensy baby toes!

Being involved in a play was the most exciting thing Snow had done since... well, since the girls' last adventure. With friends like Rose, Ella, and Rapunzel, there was always something exciting going on. But putting on a play had its own special kind of magic. The costumes, the lights, the set...

"The set!" Snow said with a gasp. She looked at the castle wall she was supposed to be working on. It was not even close to being finished! She hurriedly picked up the paintbrush she'd been using and spread the bottom of the castle with more paint. Only the paint wasn't gray like it was supposed to be. The bottom of the castle was now a brackish purple!

"Oops!" Snow instantly realized her mistake. Distracted by the scene, she had put the paintbrush in the red paint by mistake. She would have to remember to fix that later. Maybe when the purple wall was dry, she could simply cover it with a fresh coat of gray.

Snow sat back and wiped her brow, smearing it with a streak of gray. Painting sets was tricky work! She hummed to keep herself from listening to what was going on onstage. She needed to concentrate on her own work. But it wasn't long before Rose's lilting voice reached her ears, and she once again stopped to watch.

"La, la, la," Perfecta sang as she skipped across the stage. She was a young princess without a care in the world. Snow wished the princess could stop by the wings so they could skip together. How she loved to skip!

But now Perfecta was playing by a pond while that nasty Nettle watched. Snow shuddered—she wished the Scary Fairy would just leave Perfecta alone.

"Curses!" the fairy said aloud, though Perfecta didn't seem to hear him. "I might have had a chance to rule the kingdom if I hadn't been stepped upon. But thanks to that awful child—and her parents, who shunned me—I have nothing!" The Scary Fairy watched Perfecta dip her dainty toes into the pond, then buzzed furiously up behind her, ramming into her shoulder.

"Oh!" Perfecta cried, looking around to see what could have happened. But the Scary Fairy had already flown off.

Snow felt sorry for Perfecta. "Why, the poor girl has a terrible enemy and doesn't even know it!" she whispered worriedly. "Someone should warn her!"

But Snow didn't have long to think about the Scary Fairy, for the scene had already changed and Prince Gallant was galloping across the stage on his noble mount. Snow clapped her hands together, excited to see Gallant and Perfecta meet onstage. But she had forgotten that she was still holding her paintbrush, and the paint from the bristles splattered all over her hands and skirt. Luckily, Ella appeared beside her with a cleaning cloth. Snow smiled gratefully, wiped her hands and dress as best she could, and turned back to the stage.

That's strange, Snow thought as she watched Prince Gallant—Rapunzel—reach center stage. The long-haired girl began to look rather...queer. And she obviously couldn't remember her line. Luckily Ella was watching, too.

"Alas, I have seen this countryside many times over..." Snow heard Ella whisper to Rapunzel from behind the curtain.

Rapunzel cleared her throat and spoke her line, but her delivery was dismal, not at all like it had been in the cottage kitchen. And it only got worse.

Each time Prince Gallant spoke, he looked at the floor and mumbled terribly. It was painful to watch.

Poor Rapunzel seemed more like Prince Gulpy than Prince Gallant. By the time the prince was supposed to profess his undying love for the princess in the middle of Act 2, Snow was certain she had missed something. The fairy's curse was still to come, but Rapunzel already appeared to be under some sort of nasty hex. Her every move was awkward. Her every word strained. When Prince Gallant dropped to one knee to propose, he looked like he had been punched in the stomach, not overcome with love! "Goodness!" Snow exclaimed, biting a nail.

"I…" Rapunzel babbled, "…um…love you with all of my…heart," she squeaked. "Please…" She stopped and appeared unable to go on.

Rapunzel needs help! Snow thought, getting to her feet in a panic. Should she run onto the stage to rescue her friend?

No, she told herself. *Rose will know what to do.* Rose looked a bit confused but smiled sweetly down at her "prince."

Not waiting for Prince Gallant to finish the line, the Scary Fairy swooped onto the stage, a bundle of buzzing rage. "I warned you!" he bellowed. "But you foolishly chose to ignore me. Now you shall pay, and I shall rule the kingdom!"

He raised his wand, waving it before Prince Gallant.

> *You shall be mute*
> *Forevermore*
> *And lose your love*
> *Whom you adore,*

the fairy chanted.

When Gallant opened his mouth to go on, he found he could not speak!

Snow was surprised to realize that she was actually a little relieved by this development, even though she felt terribly sorry for the prince and princess. Watching

51

Rapunzel flounder for her next line had been just too awful! But how could Perfecta and Gallant marry if there was no proposal, and no acceptance? And if they didn't marry, the Scary Fairy would be next in line for the crown!

Princess Perfecta did not waste any time. She dropped to her own knee and looked her prince full in the face.

"Prince Gallant, I love you, and only you," she said plainly. "Will you be my husband?"

Prince Gallant nodded feebly, and he and the princess embraced—or rather, Rapunzel slumped into Rose's arms. But the Scary Fairy would not stand for it. He raised his wand a second time.

In order to wed
You both must be
Together with priest
And family.
So I banish prince
From princess's view.
Forever he shall
Be gone from you.

The Scary Fairy looked pointedly at Princess Perfecta. He waved his sharp wand at Prince Gallant. And in that instant, Prince Gallant disappeared.

Chapter Nine
Stage Daze

"Ooof." Rapunzel landed on a large pillow on the ground beneath the trapdoor through which she had finally escaped the stage. She expected her lurching stomach to bottom out. But, taking a deep breath, she realized that she felt totally...fine.

That's weird, she thought. Onstage she'd felt perfectly awful, like she had some strange kind of stomach bug, or had eaten something bad for breakfast. Madame Gothel, the witch who had taken her to her tower when she was just a baby, *was* known to concoct a strange meal now and again, but Rapunzel had never felt so odd in her life. She had been planning to tell Calliope that she wasn't feeling well right after her last scene, but now that she was off the stage she felt... nothing.

Oh, well, I guess that's one crisis averted, she thought with relief.

Dusting herself off, Rapunzel started to make her

way up to the auditorium when she heard Calliope make an announcement to the players.

"Nice work, everyone," Calliope said. "Particularly for a first run-through. Let's run that much again while it's still fresh in our minds. Now that the first-time jitters are out of everyone's system, things should be even better!"

Good, Rapunzel thought. Another run-through was just what she needed now that her stomach had settled.

Climbing the stairs to the stage, Rapunzel grinned and waved to Ella. Then, as the narrator read Prince Gallant's name, Rapunzel crossed the stage. She opened her mouth to speak her line, then quickly closed it to keep her breakfast in. Suddenly she felt ill *again.* What was going on? Speaking through tight lips, she managed not to sully the stage. As soon as the last word was out of her mouth she scurried into the wings of the stage holding her stomach.

Offstage, Rapunzel heaved a sigh of relief. She had done a little bit better that time, and she didn't have to go back on until the end of the first act. That would give her stomach time to settle down and quit leaping like a frog.

Stepping aside to get a better view, she watched the beginning of the play unfold. The narrator stood at stage right, telling the audience all about the birth of Princess Perfecta. They'd already rehearsed this scene today, but Rapunzel never tired of seeing it. She still chuckled over the cabbage that was momentarily playing the lead. And then there were Hagatha and Prunilla, two jesters who looked anything but jubilant. They were trying to juggle tangerines with very little success. The other actors had to be careful where they stepped so as not to slip on the pulp!

"You're terrible!" Hagatha hissed at her sister. "Go get the fruit you dropped so I can demonstrate."

"Get them yourself!" Prunilla snapped back, crossing her arms over her chest.

The townsfolk began to giggle, and the queen forgot her line altogether.

"Excellent ad-lib, jesters," Calliope called out from the audience. "But I'm afraid we need you to wait for your turn so as not to disrupt the actual dialogue in the scene."

Prunilla scrunched up her face like she'd just eaten a lemon, but said nothing. Hagatha sullenly gathered up the fallen tangerines that were still intact.

Rapunzel stepped deeper into the wings to practice her own lines. Her stomach seemed to have settled down, and she was ready to get to work. She spied Snow painting the castle set on the other side of the stage and waved a quick hello. Snow offered a supportive smile.

"You are my one true love," Rapunzel said emphatically, giving a heartfelt gaze to a giant fake tree standing in a backstage corner. It was for the country scene. "And I shall not rest until you are my very own."

Ella paused in her costume work to listen to her friend rehearse. Rapunzel wrinkled her nose. She didn't exactly like that line. It actually sounded like Princess Perfecta was something to own. She was a *person*, for goodness' sakes! She turned to watch Perfecta onstage. Rose was so talented. Rapunzel felt lucky to be cast opposite her. She just seemed so natural, and her line delivery was virtually flawless. Her intonation changed slightly with each line, and her voice carried easily across the entire auditorium.

Rapunzel quickly became engrossed in Rose's performance and almost missed her entrance altogether!

"That's your cue!" Ella whispered, coming over and thrusting the hobbyhorse into Rapunzel's hand. "It's time to meet the princess of your dreams—and capture her heart!" She gave Rapunzel a little shove.

Rapunzel climbed on the horse and galloped onto the stage. This time, she would be gallant! "Alas, I have seen this countryside many times over, but have yet to gaze upon the princess of my dreams. Indeed, I am beginning to think there is nary such a maiden for me," she said. She started off strong, but as she spoke her line she was keenly aware of the unsettled feeling growing in her stomach.

Seated beneath a willow tree, Rose looked dreamily

out toward the house. "Oh, how I wish a handsome prince would gallop into our small town and save me from this provincial existence," she said.

Rapunzel gulped as she galloped up to Rose and halted. She looked at Rose. *Focus on her eyes,* she told herself. Rapunzel stared at her friend's face, but it didn't seem to help. Rapunzel clutched her stomach and kept her mouth clamped shut.

Rose looked up at Rapunzel expectantly, her eyes slightly squinted. Was Rose trying to tell her something?

Rapunzel turned and saw Calliope out in the audience, and nearly swooned. But she steeled herself and stayed upright.

"How now, fair maiden?" Rose whispered.

Rapunzel mopped her brow. Why was it so warm in here? And why was Rose reciting her line? Oh...right.

"How now, square maiden," she mumbled. "Your lovely face must have a splendid life."

The townsfolk giggled, and Hagatha and Prunilla stopped their juggling to gawk.

Rapunzel looked helplessly at her friend. Rose pressed on as if nothing was wrong. "I have grown tired of life here in this town, though I have had a happy childhood here. I am waiting for my prince to come and take me to the ends of the earth."

Rapunzel wished Rose could take *her* to the ends of the stage and out the door. She could really use a breath of fresh air. But she had to get a handle on things. She didn't want to ruin the whole scene! Rapunzel took a deep breath. *You can do this,* she told herself. *You actually* want *to do this.*

"I believe you are, I mean...I am that prince," she said.

The next ten minutes seemed like ten years to Rapunzel, but she somehow got through her scene. Finally she exited stage right, holding her "horse" with one hand and her stomach with the other.

Handing the horse to one of the props princesses, she slumped to the floor.

"Are you all right?" Ella was at her side in an instant. "You just didn't seem yourself out there." Ella's voice was full of concern.

"I didn't feel myself out there," Rapunzel said, still clutching her stomach. Except now, suddenly, it didn't seem to need clutching. Once again she felt...normal. She looked up at Ella and decided not to say anything. Whatever was going on was weird, and she didn't want her friends to worry. They had enough to think about. Besides, she was already feeling better.

"Don't worry." Rapunzel climbed to her feet. "I'm fine," she said with a grin. She turned toward the stage—she could hear Nettle's voice carrying through the theater.

"Curses for making me only second cousin to the

queen by marriage—and twice removed at that!" he spat angrily. Rapunzel was wowed by the power of his voice. He was so tiny, and yet he filled the theater with the fury of his character. That little fairy had fire! And Rose played off it beautifully—she seemed to grow stronger with each new bit of nastiness. The two acted so well together, with such intensity, that everyone in the theater stopped to watch their scene. Nettle was on a rampage.

"You, fair Rose, shall suffer the terrible fate I have planned for you..." The Scary Fairy screamed.

Wait, Rapunzel thought. *Did he just say "Rose"? Doesn't he mean "Perfecta"?* She was certain she'd heard the name Rose come out of the fairy's mouth. He'd said it plenty loud—and Nettle *never* made mistakes. Rapunzel looked around the theater, but everyone stood watching the performance with rapt attention. If Nettle had said Rose, nobody else noticed.

Rapunzel tried to prepare herself to return to the stage. She'd felt fine while she watched the scenes she wasn't in—well, except for the creepy feeling she got when Nettle accidentally said Rose's name—and vowed to continue feeling fine. Pushing all thoughts of nausea out of her mind, she walked onto the stage with as much princely swagger as she could manage.

"What a joy is it to, uh, to..." Rapunzel fumbled over her line. *Drat.*

"See you again," Ella whispered from behind the curtain.

"Ah, yes…see you again," Rapunzel agreed. She was supposed to say something else, too—something about Rose being a feast to her eyes—but just thinking about food made her stomach heave. Her sickness was back, and with a vengeance.

She turned to look out at the audience, but that only made her feel worse. Through the swimming images of the people in the seats she thought she saw Calliope scribbling madly with her quill.

Just a little longer, Rapunzel told herself. The Scary Fairy would swoop in momentarily and make the prince mute. Then Rapunzel wouldn't have to speak at all! But she was sure she had to say several lines before then…and she had no idea what they were.

Rapunzel stepped forward, hoping that moving her feet would jog her memory.

As she walked across the stage, Rapunzel suddenly felt as though she were in a looooong hallway. The voice of Princess Perfecta echoed in her ears, but she couldn't understand what it was saying. Through the haze, Rapunzel thought she saw Nettle buzz down from the wings, a curious expression on his face.

Is that a smile? Rapunzel wondered dazedly. *Nettle never smiles!* The expression looked totally out of place. And what was Rose doing crossing the stage from the other side? She was coming toward Rapunzel, heading right over the trapdoor . . .

A second later Rapunzel saw the trapdoor open and Rose fall through. She heard a sharp cackle and several delicate gasps. And then everything went black.

Chapter Ten
The Show Must Go Wrong

Rose felt a moment of panicked confusion as her body fell downward. Did she just see Rapunzel collapse onstage? Why was she falling? And then—*thud!*—she landed on her bottom.

"Ooof!" Rose grunted. Thank goodness there was a large pillow on the ground where Rapunzel usually alighted. As it was, her landing was not very princesslike, or very soft. She gently rubbed her hindquarters. They would certainly be sore the next day.

Rose was about to get to her feet when a small crowd, including Ella and Madame Taffeta, the Princess School Stitchery teacher, scrambled down the short flight of stairs into the dim substage light. They rushed toward Rose like a stooped, stampeding hoard.

"Are you all right?" Ella asked, her face full of worry.

Rose nodded. "I'm sure I'll have a good bruise tomorrow," she said with a grimace. "But yes, I'm fine."

"You could have been seriously hurt, Briar Rose,"

62

Madame Taffeta said, her round face flushed with concern. "The trapdoor should not have unlatched in this scene. It's a wonder you didn't break a leg!"

Ella was feeling Rose's limbs for injuries. Rose felt a flash of annoyance at the teacher's concern. "I didn't break anything!" she insisted. "I'm saving that for opening night!" she joked, trying to shake off the annoyed feeling. In theater-speak "break a leg" meant "good luck." "But what happened to Rapunzel?"

"Rapunzel?" Ella echoed. She leaned in close to her friend. "Do you mean her terrible performance?" she whispered quietly.

Rose shook her head. "I thought I saw her collapse onstage just before I fell through the trapdoor."

Ella sprang to her feet and raced toward the stairs with Rose right behind her. Rose brushed the dust off her gown as she hurried after her friend. It was a fine, greenish dust. It looked like fairy dust, Rose realized. She'd seen it a hundred times. It seemed odd that there would be fairy dust underneath the stage, but she hadn't the time to think about that now. She had to get to Rapunzel!

By the time Rose and Ella (and the rest of the troupe) got back up to the stage, Rapunzel was resting in one of the house seats. She looked pale—almost as pale as Snow, who was sitting next to her, holding her hand.

"I'm fine, really," Rapunzel insisted, looking like

she wanted to race out of the auditorium. Rose knew how she felt. It was no fun being fussed over.

"I'm so glad," Rose said, pushing through the crowd and squeezing her friend's hand. "I wouldn't want to lose my prince so soon after I found him."

Rapunzel grimaced. "I'm afraid I haven't been very princelike today," she admitted.

"Never mind," Snow insisted. "You just weren't feeling well, you poor thing."

Right on cue, Madame Malady, the Princess School nurse, rushed into the auditorium. Rose was glad Rapunzel was going to get a once-over, even though she knew her friend would hate it. Rapunzel had not looked well since rehearsals started. Besides, fainting was nothing to sneeze at. But Madame Malady rushed past Rapunzel and right up to *Rose* instead.

"Are you all right, dear?" she asked, her birdlike hands grasping Rose's arm.

Rose straightened and curtsied. "I'm fine, Madame," she said. "It's Rapunzel you may wish to inquire after."

Rapunzel shot Rose a look, but Rose held firm. She had to do what was best for her friend. "She fainted just moments ago."

"Fainted!" the nurse echoed. "Well, she certainly won't be at rehearsal for the next day or two." She helped Rapunzel to her feet and, very slowly, led her up the pink-carpeted aisle to the main corridor. "Oh, dear. How many fingers am I holding…" Her voice disappeared as the door closed quietly behind her.

As soon as Rapunzel was gone, princesses all around Rose began to whisper fretfully to one another.

"Fainted!" one said.

"Worse than sitting on a pea!" said another.

"And what about what happened to poor Beauty?" added a third. "It's almost like our play is cursed!"

Rose ignored the hubbub and turned her attention to Calliope. She hoped the director had a plan for Rapunzel's absence. In spite of her friend's shaky performance, Rose felt sad to see her go.

"All right, all right," Calliope said. "We must get back to our rehearsing. The show must go on!" She scanned the group of princesses before her. "We'll need a temporary Prince Gallant, of course. Snow White, how would you like to fill in?"

"Oooooh!" Snow cried, unable to contain her excitement. "I'd just love to!"

"Fine." Calliope nodded, her black curls bobbing on her back. "Let's get started, then. We'll begin at the beginning of Act 2. Places, everyone. And quickly."

Rose took her place on stage and tried to stay focused. She was worried about Rapunzel!

Backstage, Ella handed Snow the horse, and Snow

straddled the wooden pole. Then she skipped joyfully onto the stage, trotting around and around until she was almost dizzy.

"What a joy it is to ride this lovely horsey...I mean, to see your lovely face again," Snow crooned to Rose. "Your face is like a feast to my hungry eyes."

She stopped skipping, hopped off the horse, and stood before Rose, gazing at her with her round ebony eyes.

Rose giggled, then remembered she was playing a part. She had to stay in character! She gazed up at Snow as if she were a dashing prince and not her wonderful, innocent friend. After all, Princess Perfecta and Prince Gallant were about to be engaged!

Chapter Eleven
Curtains for Rose

Ella's needle darted swiftly in and out of the fabric she was stitching like a hummingbird sipping nectar from a trumpet vine. She could almost sew without looking—thanks to all the mending she was forced to do at home—which allowed her to keep up with her costume work and follow everything that was happening onstage at the same time.

Eagerly, Ella watched the third act. She had seen Rose perform it at least a dozen times over the past week, but she never tired of it. For almost the entire act Rose was alone in the stage lights. The finale was her time to shine—the part when Princess Perfecta stopped giving orders and took matters into her own hands.

The beginning of the third act is what makes the role of Perfecta so perfect for Rose, Ella thought as she threaded her needle. Before the final curtain, Princess Perfecta would solve her problems all on her own to create the happily ever after she dreamed of. Rose's performance was truly inspiring. But the part Ella liked best, the part she always waited for, was the final conflict between Princess Perfecta and the Scary Fairy. The very last scene was the most thrilling part of the whole show. It never failed to capture Ella's full attention.

Overall, the play was in great shape. Whole sections of it, like the third act, were practically polished. But there were a few scenes that still had Ella worried—mostly the scenes with Rapunzel in them. Ella glanced nervously across the stage at where her long-haired friend was waiting to go on for her final scene. It hadn't helped that Rapunzel had gotten ill and had to miss two days of rehearsal. She was the player most in need of rehearsal, but now she would have the *least* time to practice. When she'd come back this morning, it looked like the rest had done her good, but gazing at her now, Ella was fearful of a relapse. Rapunzel seemed dazed and forgetful. She wasn't acting much like a prince. She wasn't acting much like herself, either. Her gusto was simply gone.

Maybe I can help, Ella thought. She tied off her stitches, took her sewing, and made her way behind the scenery to the other side of the stage where Rapunzel was sitting. "Do you want to run lines?" Ella offered in a whisper. "You probably didn't have much energy for memorizing while you were recuperating." Ella tried to explain away Rapunzel's lackluster performance.

"Actually, I felt fine at home. And I knew my lines by heart." Rapunzel shook her head. She looked positively baffled. "I felt so good, Mother Gothel and I did nothing but run lines for two days. I could recite them in my sleep." Rapunzel's expression suddenly changed to one of amusement. "I wish you could have seen Mother Gothel doing the Scary Fairy. She could give Nettle a run for his money!" Rapunzel grinned at Ella. Then her smile faded. "I guess I'm just having a little relapse." Rapunzel grimaced toward the stage. "It's so strange, it's really only when I'm—"

Suddenly, Rapunzel went silent. She'd heard her cue. It was time for her to go on. She stood motionless with an odd look on her face until Ella gave her a nudge.

"Prepare to be rescued by your true love, Prince Gallant." Ella smiled encouragingly at Rapunzel before the poor girl stumbled out onto the stage.

Well, she does look cursed, Ella thought. Rapunzel kept mopping her brow with her sleeve, and her face was becoming an odd shade of green. She looked like a prince turning into a frog. Not very gallant at all.

Thank goodness she has Perfecta to rescue her, Ella thought, *and that she's supposed to be mute in their scene.* Rapunzel seemed almost as ill as she had the day she'd fainted. But at least today she remained upright.

"I will not be victim to your jealousy and your hate,"

69

Princess Perfecta said defiantly as she burst into the Scary Fairy's lair.

"You cannot remove the curse!" the Scary Fairy bellowed.

"Yes, I can," Perfecta replied evenly. "For I am filled with love for my handsome prince, mute or no. And love is stronger than hate."

When the scene ended, Ella breathed a sigh of relief. Rapunzel had made it through. And Rose had been terrific! The cast and crew clapped wildly as the curtain closed. Then everyone gathered to hear notes about their performance from Calliope. Rapunzel sat at the edge of the stage, the natural color slowly returning to her face.

Ella found a seat by Snow in the audience and kept right on sewing.

Calliope was gathering her thoughts and her very long scroll when Rose walked onto the stage, where most of the rest of the cast was already gathered. The director dropped what she was doing, stood, and began to clap loudly. The townsfolk joined in the applause and soon all of the princesses and players in the room were clapping for Rose.

Ella smiled broadly at her friend. Rose was getting a standing ovation! And she deserved it. Of course, Rose demurred. She bowed her head humbly and spoke soft words of thanks.

At that moment Nettle buzzed onto the stage and hovered behind Rose. Ella noticed him glaring at the back of Rose's head just as he always did as the Scary Fairy. Ella wondered if the spiky little sprite ever broke character.

"Rapunzel," Calliope began, "it's good to have you back."

Ella agreed. Snow had been enthusiastic about filling in, but she'd been unable to contain her giggles and ebullient exclamations. Ella smiled to herself remembering Snow's performance. Her raven-haired friend could pull off sweet in spades, but not gallant.

"We'll need to spend a little more time on your scenes," Calliope went on, addressing Rapunzel. "We want to make sure you are prepared for opening night." Ella knew Calliope was trying not to overwhelm Rapunzel. She also knew "a little more time" was an understatement. Rapunzel just nodded.

"Rose." Calliope moved to the next cast member on her scroll. "Rose, you are blossoming into an actress before our eyes! You are truly captivating onstage," Calliope cooed.

"She really is!" Snow leaned closer to Ella, nodding her paint-spattered head. Snow wasn't the only one nodding in agreement. Everyone seemed to think Rose was stupendous. Only Nettle gave Rose a withering look.

Maybe, Ella thought, *he's jealous.* She waited for

Calliope to get to Nettle's notes. She thought when Calliope told him that he, too, was doing a wonderful job he might stop glaring—he might even smile. But Calliope moved from cast to crew without a mention of the fairy's name. Ella thought it was strange. Nettle was obviously a great actor. He was utterly convincing, and Rose was always saying she was learning so much from him. Perhaps Calliope didn't think he needed the same kind of encouragement as the students. After all, he was already a real player. Still, Ella thought, everybody needs some positive feedback—and maybe a few compliments would improve Nettle's mood. If he weren't so prickly, she would tell him herself.

When Calliope dismissed the group, Ella watched Nettle dart away, up toward the catwalk and the riggings where the hanging lanterns, set pieces, and curtains were hung. She felt bad for the prickly pixie. She knew a single kind word could go a long way.

Packing up her sewing and stifling a yawn, Ella waited for Rapunzel and Rose. Rapunzel slid off the edge of the stage, looking better all the time. But Rose was busy talking to the townsfolk. They swarmed around her like ducklings around a crust of bread, eager to pay her a compliment.

At last the crowd dispersed, leaving Rose alone and looking exhausted. Ella waved. She wanted to catch

Rose's eye, but suddenly something high above it all caught Ella's eye instead.

Ella screamed. The stage was bathed in red as the heavy theater curtain dropped like a lead weight, knocking Rose to the floor.

Chapter Twelve
Seeing Red

One moment Rose had been standing on the stage and the next she was pressed to the ground. Someone had screamed. Had it been her? She felt a tremendous weight holding her flat to the ground. She opened her eyes. Everything was red. She was swimming in a sea of crimson velvet.

Rose reached out in two directions, searching for the edge of the enormous stage curtain. She could hear muffled voices on the other side, calling her name.

"Rose!" Snow and Ella were the first to reach their friend, with Rapunzel close behind. They pulled back the heavy curtain and helped her to her feet. "Are you all right?"

Rose squinted into the bright stage light. Nearly the entire cast and crew had gathered around her, and when she nodded that she was fine there were many gasps and a smattering of applause.

"Tender Rose!" one of the townsfolk cried. "How could we let this happen to our star?"

"Everyone listen. We must watch out for Beauty. This is the second time in a week she has been in an accident." A Crown Rose vaguely recognized was rallying the group into a worried frenzy.

"Don't accidents always happen in threes?" another voice asked.

"We've got to keep Beauty safe. It's almost opening night!" A chorus of townsfolk murmured their agreement.

Rose rolled her eyes and looked at her friends for help. She had to get out of there! She had hoped that the play would give her a chance to avoid the constant fuss she usually attracted and here it was actually creating more. The added attention felt more suffocating than the heavy curtain that had nearly crushed her.

With a nod, Ella indicated a rarely used door to the left of the stage that led directly outside. As usual she knew without speaking what her friend needed most. "You're sure you're okay?" she whispered.

"I will be! I just need a few minutes alone." Rose ducked between Rapunzel and Snow and raced out the side exit into the cold. She didn't have her cloak, or even her script. But she didn't care. She took a deep breath and blew it out in a billowing cloud.

Outside, the world was a white and silent winter wonderland. It was freezing cold, and to Rose, it was bliss. Slowly she began to make her way to the front of the castle where she knew her coach would be waiting.

She was about to round the front turret when she saw something swooping low to the ground out of the corner of her eye. It was too early for swallows. And the blur was purplish green. Nettle!

Rose hurried to catch up with her costar. Lately it seemed that the grumpy fairy was the only person who was not trying to coddle her like a cooked egg. Rose preferred his aloofness to the other cast members' nonstop compliments and fawning. She had been trying to tell him for quite some time what an acting inspiration he was as well—she hoped this would be her chance. But by the time she got to the front of the school he was gone.

Instead of one crabby dark fairy Rose saw seven bright sprites. Rose's colorful guardian fairies were like a rainbow against the snow. They were swarming together near the coach, waiting for her. When they spotted her standing in the cold with no wrap and no boots, they buzzed around her like tiny townsfolk, hurrying her into the coach.

"You'll catch your death!"

"What were you thinking?"

"I wasn't thinking," Rose said, trying to wave them off. "After the curtain fell on me I just wanted to get away." The fairies were suddenly still. Rose looked at their worried faces. Ugh. She had blown it. She should not have mentioned the curtain accident.

"I'm fine!" she insisted, but that just set them off even more. Petunia and Tulip buzzed around her head checking for bruises. Buttercup hovered in her face, a blur of concern and yellow wings, looking from eye to eye.

"Just as we suspected." Pansy folded her tiny arms. "It was Nettle, wasn't it?"

"We never should have let her go back onstage after the first incident," Daisy squeaked. "We're lucky she hasn't been killed."

"I told you that Nettle was up to no good!" Petunia kicked out her leg, putting her foot down in midair. "He clearly has it out for Rose."

Rose leaned back against the velvet seat and shut her eyes. She had no idea why her fairies thought the accidents were Nettle's fault, but she knew there was nothing she could say that would convince them otherwise. She hadn't seen the fairies in this much of a dither in quite a while, and she knew things were going to get worse before they got better.

* * *

"Briar Rose! Come to dinner this instant!" Rose's father bellowed from the foot of the castle stairs later that night. It was the moment Rose had been dreading. Bracing herself, she walked slowly down the stairs to the evening meal. She plastered a pleasant smile across her face.

"Good evening, Father. Good evening, Mother," she greeted her parents politely. Rose knew there was no avoiding the coming tempest, but it was worth a try. She slid into her seat across from King Hector and Queen Margaret and delicately took a bite of her bread as if nothing was the matter.

Her father looked as cooked as the goose on the table. His lips trembled as he tried to remain composed. "Rose dear, why haven't you told us about the perils of playacting? We heard from your guardian fairies that you have nearly been killed upon the stage!"

"Twice!" Rose's mother gasped. She looked positively peaked.

Rose took a deep breath. Talk about dramatic! Didn't anyone think she could take care of herself? "I did not almost die," Rose said calmly. "I admit that there has been a mishap or two, but it was nothing serious. Please, Mother, don't fret. I am fine." Rose turned back to her first course, hoping that would be the end of the discussion, knowing it was just the beginning.

"This is not acceptable," King Hector said. "Others may have mishaps, but not you, my fair Rose. I simply will not allow it. As such, your mother and I shall be going to see the headmistress first thing in the morning." King Hector glanced from his wife to his daughter and back again as he spoke, as if he was waiting for one of them to stop him. "We are going to ask that you be removed from the play at once. It is far too dangerous for one who is as—"

"For one who is as *what*?" Rose couldn't keep quiet any longer. "For one who is enjoying herself as much as I? For one who is working this hard to make you proud?" She would not give up the play. She would not! She had too much of her heart in it—and she was not about to let down the rest of the cast, the crew, or Calliope.

Rose jumped up from her seat. She was planning to storm out, run up to her room, slam the door, and sulk. Then she thought better of it.

"I'm sorry." Rose sank back into her cushioned seat. "Please forgive my outburst."

The king and queen exchanged glances.

"But do hear me out," Rose continued. "I am enjoying this play more than anything I have ever done. I think I've finally found something I'm good at."

"But darling, you are good at *everything*!" Rose's mother burbled.

"This is different," Rose said. There were no right words to explain how she felt when she was onstage. She switched tactics. "If you don't allow me to try new things, to take a few risks, you might as well lock me in a tower." Rose's parents had been horrified when they learned about how Rapunzel had been brought up. "Or just put me to sleep until it's time for me to be married."

"Dearest, we would never—"

Rose put up her hand to stop her father. "Please let me do this," she said quietly.

The king and queen were quiet. They looked at their laps and then into their daughter's eyes.

"Will you wear armor?" the king asked.

Rose shook her head and bit her tongue.

"Will you be careful?" the queen asked.

"Of course," Rose answered.

Slowly, the king and queen nodded their assent.

Rose jumped to her feet and hugged each of her parents in turn. "And please," Rose added, "promise me you'll keep those meddling fairies away until opening night!"

Chapter Thirteen
Acting Funny

Ella burst out of the coach, took a deep breath of the crisp morning air, and practically ran across the bridge to school. Although it was nice to get a ride each morning, sitting in the tiny coach compartment with her quarreling steps was getting unbearable. And being forced to rehearse with them was even worse!

"Cinderella! Get back here! Help me down!" Hagatha barked behind her. Ella didn't turn to look. Let the coachman help. She could not stand to be near them for another minute.

For a day or two Ella had gotten a break from rehearsing with Hagatha and Prunilla while they pouted about their parts. But all too soon they had realized that they could get just as much attention for playing the fools as they could for playing pretty and charming. *Probably more*, Ella thought, because being pretty and charming would require acting skills they simply didn't have. But ever since they had decided to embrace their comedic roles, Hag and Prune had done nothing but fight over who had the funniest lines. It made Ella's head throb.

"Punch is far more amusing. That's why Calliope cast me," Ella heard Prunilla brag as the coach pulled away.

"No, Foil's the funnier of the two," Hagatha retorted. "I'm the one who gets the real laughs."

Ella rolled her eyes. It was only a matter of time before the sisters would start stomping toes and scratching faces...again.

Thankfully that was all Ella heard before the Princess School doors shut behind her. She hurried to her velvet-lined trunk to collect her sewing. She would be able to get loads done on the costumes this morning, and maybe getting things done would help quiet the worries whirling in her head.

They had come to school early to give Hagatha and Prunilla extra rehearsal time. It was getting close to opening night, and there were still some kinks to work out in their scenes. But it wasn't just her stepsisters' scenes that were problematic, Ella knew. Rapunzel had stayed late the day before and was scheduled to come in early this morning, too. Ella hoped her friend was feeling better. Rapunzel's stomach bug seemed unrelenting. Just when everyone thought she was better she would get sick again! Not even Madame Malady could explain it.

Ella's mind flashed to Madame Gothel. Could the old witch be sabotaging Rapunzel's efforts at acting? Rapunzel's foster mother had tried to keep Rapunzel from Princess School before...but lately Rapunzel had only sweet things to say about her. She had even been helping Rapunzel practice. No, it had to be something else.

After gathering several yards of brightly colored fabric and two pairs of plain slippers, Ella walked to the auditorium and settled in the last row of seats to watch what was happening onstage while she worked.

Rapunzel, Hag, and Prune weren't the only thing troubling Ella about *The Tale of the Scary Fairy*. Nettle, the Scary Fairy himself, had been on her mind as well. He was a frighteningly good actor. He was also downright frightening, and Ella suspected he might have something to do with the mishaps surrounding Rose. Rose had arrived the day before in an outrage because her parents had tried to stop her from doing the play. Though she would never say so to Rose, Ella secretly wondered if they were right to be scared.

I'll just keep my eye on things, Ella thought as she sewed a large jingle bell onto the toe of one slipper. *Make sure there are no more accidents.*

Onstage, Hagatha and Prunilla were stumbling about, searching for Prince Gallant.

"This way!" Hagatha grunted, pulling on Prunilla's arm with all her might.

"That way!" Prunilla strained in the other direction, shaking free of Hagatha's grasp and sending her sister sprawling.

"Stop! Please!" Calliope was no longer laughing. "Could you please say your lines, just one time through, the way they were written?" She sounded exasperated, and Ella could understand why. Ella herself had wondered why she worked so hard to help her steps remember their lines when they never managed to say them onstage. They just argued their way through every scene, making it up as they went. Though, Ella had to admit, from out here in the theater seats it was rather funny.

Ella was finishing the slippers when players and princesses began to arrive. Crew members bustled busily backstage. Most of the set pieces were ready and the props had been gathered, but there were lots and lots of final details to attend to. And today they were going to have their first full run-through—it would be a sneak preview of sorts for the regular Princess School instructors. Everyone wanted it to go well.

"Oh, there you are!" Snow skipped up to Ella, out of breath. "I wanted to come early, too, but the dwarves didn't want to wake me. They said I was sleeping so peacefully they even made their own porridge this morning!" Snow picked up one of the silly slippers and admired Ella's handiwork. "These are adorable, Ella! You are almost done and I still have so much to do!"

Snow was talking so fast Ella could not get a word in.

"I accidentally painted part of the castle purple — a lovely shade, like a ripe plum — but not the right color for a castle. Now I have to redo it. And I want to try something new beneath the windows, too..." Snow kept talking as she walked off to find her paint and brushes. Ella watched her push past the throng of townsfolk who were all burbling about something near the stage.

"Oh, dear!" With a gasp, Ella realized the townsfolk had Rose surrounded, and she'd only just arrived! Ella knew that was the last thing Rose needed today.

"Watch your step, Beauty!" one of them said as she took Rose's elbow to help her over the lip of carpet running down the aisle. Rose shook free only to be flanked by three or four more girls offering to help her with the stairs. After the accidents with the trapdoor and the curtain, the townsfolk had taken it upon themselves to protect Princess Perfecta until the play opened — much to Rose's dismay.

Setting down the red neck ruffle she'd just started

stitching, Ella stood to see what she could do to rescue her friend. Standing on the tips of her toes, she caught a glimpse of Rose in the cluster of girls. The look on her face said it all. Nothing irritated Rose more than a fuss.

Ella was looking for a way through the crowd when Calliope clapped her hands together onstage and called for Prince Gallant. Hagatha and Prunilla had made it to the end of their scene at last and it was time to prepare for the run-through.

Looking around, Ella suddenly realized that she had not seen Rapunzel yet even though she was supposed to have come in early. Someone needed to look for her. It wasn't going to be Rose—she was trapped by admirers. And it wasn't going to be Snow, either. She was standing onstage looking at her purple castle wall and chewing on the end of her brush. It was up to Ella to find her.

With an apologetic wave to Rose, Ella turned back down the aisle and headed for the door. She had an idea where Rapunzel might be.

The stable doors opened with a creak. Inside it was dry and warmer, though Ella could still see her breath. She breathed heavily after her run through the snowy gardens. "Rapunzel?" she panted. "Are you here?"

The pigeons fluttered in the rafters, and one of the

horses pawed the ground. Then it was silent. Ella was about to turn back when she heard a feeble voice.

"Over here."

Rapunzel was splayed across a bale of hay inside an empty stall. She looked paler than Ella had ever seen her—even her freckles were white. And she was shaking.

Ella rushed to her side. "Oh, Rapunzel," she said softly. "You poor thing! Should I go fetch Madame Malady?"

Rapunzel shook her head and mumbled something Ella didn't catch into the bale of hay.

"Pardon me. What was that?" Ella asked gently, helping Rapunzel sit up.

"I've figured it out," Rapunzel repeated. "I'm not sick. It's stage fright. I mean, I have stage fright. I wasn't sick. I mean, I am sick, but only when I have to go onstage." She looked almost embarrassed. "I can't do this."

Ella gave Rapunzel a quick hug. "Of course you can! Rapunzel, listen to me—you're a perfect Prince Gallant. I know you can do it because I saw you practice in Snow's cottage."

Rapunzel shook her head. "That was different. When I'm onstage, my stomach starts churning and I forget all my lines."

"I'll help you," Ella promised. "You only have to get through it two more times. If you need a little help, just cock an ear stage right. I'll be right there with your lines."

Rapunzel took a deep breath. "Okay," she said finally, swallowing hard. "Two more times. Just...don't tell anyone, okay?" Ella knew that Rapunzel hated to appear weak.

Ella looked Rapunzel in the eyes, nodded, and gave her shoulders a squeeze. "You can do this," she told her. She just hoped she was right.

Chapter Fourteen

What's the Buzz About?

Snow hummed quietly to herself. Sometimes humming helped her keep her mind on what she needed to do. And what she needed to do now was finish painting this set! Onstage the dress rehearsal was beginning, and Snow would have liked nothing more than to watch the whole play from beginning to end, but she was going to have to wait until opening night for that. After she was done correcting the castle wall, she planned to paint flower boxes under all of the windows. Snow smiled to herself. Flowers always reminded her of her father.

Snow covered her purple wall with gray, adding splashes of darker gray and brown to make the stones. Maybe she would paint a climbing vine or two when she was finished. She just couldn't resist adding the extra color.

Snow dipped her brush in a bucket of paint. She stopped humming while she worked on the edge.

She did not want to drip. But the humming in her ears did not go away.

That's funny, Snow thought, taking her brush off the canvas. *I was quite sure I stopped humming a moment ago.* Confused, Snow turned around...and spotted the source of the hum. It was not coming from her at all—it was the rapidly beating wings of Rose's fairies!

"Hello!" Snow chirped. "Have you come for the dress rehearsal?" Snow simply adored Rose's fairies. They reminded her of her dwarves, only lovelier, tinier, and quite a bit more colorful. They were like friendly flying flowers. But not one of them responded to her greeting. They were hovering in a tight circle and all seemed to be talking at once.

They must not have heard me, Snow thought. She waved her arm to try to catch their attention, dripping paint onto her hair and clothes. *Rose's fairies would never be unfriendly. Not like that Nettle.* The moment Snow thought about Nettle she heard the name echoed. It was as if the fairies had read her mind...no, they were talking about Nettle already!

It was not polite to eavesdrop, Snow knew, but she could not help it. She was curious about what the fairies had to say about the little grouch.

"It was so long ago." Tulip shook her tiny red head sadly. "I can't believe that Nettle still holds a grudge."

"He's not like the rest of us," Daisy said. "It's really not his fault. He has had a nasty sting ever since he was born."

"It must be hard to be Nettle." Buttercup sighed.

Snow blinked. Her wide eyes grew wider. Slowly she began to understand that Nettle was a flower fairy, like the others, but his flower power was not that of a pretty daisy or buttercup. *Of course.* It was beginning to make sense. Nettle was named for the stinging nettles that grew wild in the woods. Snow knew about stinging nettles because she gathered them each spring. When cooked, they were a powerful medicine. But she could only gather them while wearing heavy gloves. If she touched them barehanded they would sting her skin and leave a mark that lasted for days. It sounded like Nettle was similarly untouchable—which explained why he always wore gloves himself.

"No one could ever hug him. He was far too sharp," Viola said sadly. "It's no wonder the king and queen were afraid to allow him near their baby. But perhaps they should not have banished him from the castle."

Snow's eyes welled up with tears when she imagined a little fairy going unhugged. But what was that about banishing from the castle? Could they be talking about Rose's parents?

"That's no excuse for threatening Briar Rose! Nettle

is a powerful fairy and we can't let Rose come to harm. If he casts a curse…" Pansy pounded her tiny purple fist in her palm. Her wings were a blur behind her.

Did she say "curse"? Snow shuddered. Her tears dried up immediately. Curses were serious business. For a moment Snow was frozen. The fairies, too, were quiet, hovering and wringing their tiny hands. Then with a *plunk* Snow dropped her brush, splattering paint as the threat sank in. Rose was in danger.

Snow leaped to her feet, knocking over paint cans and leaving a colorful trail of footprints all the way to where Ella was standing in the wings watching the dress rehearsal.

Ella grinned at the sight of Snow covered in paint, but her expression quickly changed. Snow knew that Ella had guessed that something was wrong.

"Is it Rapunzel?" Ella whispered. "She made it through her first scene oka—" Ella trailed off when Snow interrupted, shaking her head.

"It's Rose! She's in danger!" Snow whispered frantically. "Real danger!"

Ella listened carefully as Snow whispered everything she'd overheard into Ella's ear as they waited for Rose to come offstage. It took all of the pale princess's will not to interrupt the scene, drag Rose back to her cottage, and lock the doors.

The moment Rose came off, Snow threw her arms

around her, nearly knocking her back onstage. "We have to protect you!" she cried. "You're in danger—Nettle wants to curse you. I heard it from your fairies!"

Rose looked a little shocked at first. Then she just looked annoyed. She shrugged out of Snow's embrace.

"Where have I heard *that* before?" she smirked. "You say the fairies are *here*?" Rose's frown deepened. "They promised," she muttered.

Then her eyes flashed back on Snow and Ella. "I'm used to my fairies, and my parents, and my teachers, and even the townsfolk being overprotective, but do you have to start with it, too?" she said accusingly.

The reproach in Rose's eyes was shocking. Snow stumbled back. Didn't Rose realize the danger was real?

"Just tell me where the fairies are," Rose demanded.

Snow had never seen Rose so angry before. She felt a little scared to speak, so she simply pointed to the set room where she had been painting and watched agape as Rose turned and stomped off in that direction.

Chapter Fifteen
Moment of Truth

Rose strode toward the set room in a fit of fury. This was the last straw. Did her friends have to be worrywart alarmists as well? It was like a terrible, contagious disease. And *only* Rapunzel was immune.

But she has her own illness to cope with, Rose thought, setting her jaw. She hoped Rapunzel's stomach bug wasn't catching. More than that, she hoped Rapunzel would feel better—and *act* better—soon. And more than anything she hoped everyone would just stop worrying and leave her alone.

Passing by the prop room, Rose plucked a small butterfly net from the wall. She tiptoed to the door of the set room. She needn't have worried about being quiet. The fairies were still buzzing in a ring. With a flick of her wrist Rose captured them all. They tumbled together in a colorful clump while Rose held the mesh sack closed at the top with her fist.

94

"Rose!" The fairies all talked at once, trying to explain what they were doing there. But Rose tuned them out until they were just a ringing in her ears.

"You promised to stay away until opening night," she said calmly. "I'm just going to make sure that you do." Rose marched back to the prop room. Taking a large lantern down from a hook, she opened the glass door and dumped her tiny guardians inside. "I will let you out as soon as it is time to go home," Rose whispered hoarsely. "In the meantime, no meddling!"

The fairies protested as loudly as they could, but even with their voices joined together the noise was only a resonant hum. Spying a piece of cloth, Rose dropped it over the fairy cage, further dampening their pleas before hanging the big lantern back on its hook.

A twinge of guilt tugged at Rose's heart. She glanced back once at the swaying lantern before running back to the stage wings. She did not want to miss her next entrance. She had made it through the painful Prince Gallant scenes and the awkward Punch and Foil scenes. Her favorite part was coming up.

Rose pushed all thoughts of meddling fairies, parents, friends, and danger from her mind. She took a deep breath and tried to imagine herself as Princess Perfecta. Rose's anger left her, replaced by Perfecta's sadness and longing for her true love. Then Rose felt

Perfecta's frustration. The princess had given order after order to try to bring her prince back—only to come up shorthanded.

Taking the stage, Rose paced the castle room and lamented loudly before the audience, "What good is it to issue orders if no one can fulfill them? My demands have cost me dearly. And now only one option remains."

Rose felt her own resolve and determination grow stronger along with Perfecta's. She dusted off her dainty hands. She hoisted her heavy skirts. She did not need help. "I will find my love myself," she announced.

As the scene changed, new set pieces slid onto the stage. Stagehands threw sand and water and fake snowflakes from the wings as Princess Perfecta fought her way through terrible storms and dangerous landscapes. Nothing could keep Perfecta from finding her love.

Rose reveled in her role and felt triumph with each step. The whole play turned when Princess Perfecta took things into her own hands. But the show was not over yet.

With a final gasp, Perfecta climbed up a craggy constructed hillside. The Scary Fairy was waiting on the other side.

Nettle hovered ominously over Rapunzel. Both of them were perfectly in character. Rapunzel was limp and mute, a cursed prince, and Nettle was angry and threatening. Behind them Hem, Haw, Punch, Foil, and the king and queen were tied up and gagged. Though almost the entire cast was onstage, this scene was between Nettle and Rose alone.

"What good can you do here, pretty princess?" the Scary Fairy spat mockingly.

Rose recoiled slightly. Nettle sounded even more venomous than usual. "More good than you can ever know." She spoke her line clearly. As Perfecta, she was supposed to feel angry at the evil sprite. But Rose had to struggle to suppress her admiration—Nettle's hatred for her seemed so real! He was truly an extraordinary actor. But she was Princess Perfecta now, not Rose. And she was seeking revenge. There would be time to tell Nettle how she felt when the scene was over.

Snapping back into character, Rose stared evenly at the Scary Fairy. "Love is stronger than hate," she said, pulling a sword from her belt. She deftly cut the binding off the captured prince and tied one around the fairy's wings. She was victorious!

"You have rescued me, my love," Rapunzel said, getting slowly to her feet. "The curse is broken." She looked feeble. But she did manage to utter her last lines before the curtain was lowered.

Rose could hear the teachers and students in the audience applauding loudly. Then the curtain rose, and the cast took their bows. A couple of princesses threw bouquets to Rose, and though she did not believe she was the best on the stage, she could not deny the loudest applause was for her. Grasping hands, the whole cast bowed once more before exiting.

Rose looked across the stage at Rapunzel. She looked awful. *Maybe I should find Madame Malady,* Rose thought. Then something else caught her eye—a green-and-purple blur. Nettle. He buzzed off the stage and into the dressing room.

This was her chance to finally tell him how much his performance, and his presence, inspired her. How much it meant to have the chance to work with him.

Rose slipped away from the crowd of cast members onstage and peeked into the dressing room. She was relieved to see that Nettle was by himself. He hovered in a corner, his back turned. As she lifted her fist to knock on the nearly closed door she realized the fairy was talking to himself. Rose couldn't believe he was still running lines. His performance was already perfect! She stood quietly to listen, and as she did her jaw dropped. Nettle was not reciting lines, he was chanting.

A curse I cast, a thorny spell.
Blooming Rose, all love thee well.

The curtain shall rise, the audience adore,
But their sleeping Beauty will wake no more.

Rose's heart hammered in her chest. She backed noiselessly away from the door. Snow and her fairies were right. Rose *was* in danger. She had just been cursed!

Chapter Sixteen

The Show Must Go On

Rose's hand flew to her face as she turned and ran away from the dressing room. Reeling from her alarming discovery, Rose found a quiet corner backstage and slumped to the ground. She needed time and space to think.

Taking several deep breaths, Rose tried to calm down. Emotions collided within her. She felt guilty that she hadn't believed those who were trying—with good reason—to protect her! And she was embarrassed that she'd had no idea what was happening. She had spent her whole life believing that the danger others worried about did not exist. And now, suddenly, it was right here! When the curtain rose on opening night, the audience's adoration of Rose would trigger Nettle's curse...and she would "wake no more."

Thank goodness it's just me he's cursed and not the whole cast, Rose thought. She was grateful that ignoring the warnings hadn't put anyone else in harm's way.

From her little backstage corner, Rose looked at the results of the players' and crew's hard work. The sets were built, painted, and ready—they looked great. The costumes were colorful, creative, and finely sewn. Everyone had worked hard, and they had come so far...and now Nettle was planning to ruin it all.

All of a sudden Rose was mad. How could Nettle do this?! Well, he wouldn't. Rose wouldn't let him. Because there was one emotion she was not feeling: fear. Rose was not afraid of Nettle.

Rose quickly got to her feet. She had to find her friends! She crossed to the other side of the stage and found Ella, Snow, and Rapunzel in a huddle. Rose rushed up to them and squeezed Rapunzel's and Snow's hands. "We have to talk," she whispered, looking around and cocking an ear to make sure Nettle wasn't hovering nearby. That little fairy was sneaky.

Rose led her friends to a corner and turned back to face them. They all stared at her, silent, their eyes wide. They were ready to hear what she had to say. "I've been cursed," she whispered. "By Nettle." She explained what she'd overheard outside the dressing room door.

Snow's eyes got wider and wider as Rose spoke. Ella shook her head slightly. And Rapunzel looked more like herself than she had in days.

"That evil little bug," Rapunzel said, her eyes bright. She looked feisty and ready for a fight.

"Snow, I'm sorry I didn't listen to you," Rose said. "I know you were just trying to keep me safe, and I shouldn't have gotten so angry. It's just that, well, usually the danger everyone is always warning me about doesn't exist."

"Well, it does now," Ella said worriedly. "What are we going to do?"

"I'm not sure," Rose admitted. "Nettle is obviously pretty powerful—much more so than my…my fairies!" Rose exclaimed, her hand flying to her mouth. How could she have forgotten about her fairies? She raced toward the prop area. "I've left them locked up!" she called back to her friends.

Ella, Snow, and Rapunzel hurried after her. By the time they got to the prop table Rose was already releasing the fairies from the hanging lantern.

"It's about time," Petunia complained, glaring at Rose and brushing fairy dust off her skirts.

"We thought you were going to leave us in there for eternity," Daisy added.

"That really was not appropriate, Rose," Pansy said, hovering right in front of Rose's face. "We are not your possessions. We are your guardians."

Rose sighed. "I know," she said. "I'm sorry. I should not have let my temper get the best of me. I've been wretched and ungrateful. Please, please forgive me!"

"Of course we do, dear," Tulip said softly.

"If you promise not to do it again," Petunia insisted.

"Of course I promise," Rose said. "And, uh, there's something we need to discuss. I overheard Nettle casting a spell on me for opening night."

"What?"

"Oh, no!"

"How dreadful!"

"It's exactly what we feared!"

The fairies all spoke at the same time. Rose had never seen them so upset.

"We must alert your father at once!" Buttercup cried breathlessly.

"No," Rose said calmly. "I want to deal with Nettle myself. If we tell my parents, they will have every theater in the kingdom shut down. Everyone at Princess School has worked terribly hard on this production—it would be awful to cancel it because of me and a little curse."

"But what if it isn't so little?" Snow asked, her voice a little shaky. "How can we outsmart a wicked fairy?"

Rapunzel stood straight, her shoulders squared. She looked like...Rapunzel. "Together." She eyed the flock of fairies still buzzing around somewhat scatteredly. "All of us."

"There is something we fairies can do," Daisy said thoughtfully. She buzzed up to Pansy and whispered in her ear.

"Yes, yes," Pansy replied, looking around warily. "But we must go to the coach."

Minutes later, Rose, Rapunzel, Snow, Ella, and the seven fairies climbed into Rose's coach. Rose felt relief wash over her when they were all inside and the door had been closed. They were alone for certain now. Rose leaned back against the plush velvet cushion and spread a warm woolen blanket over all of their laps to ward off the chill.

The fairies wasted no time in getting to work. They joined hands, forming a colorful, hovering circle. Then, in their tiny voices, they began to chant.

Nettle's curse.
We must reverse.
The audience adore,
Sweet Rose forevermore.

They repeated the chant three times, their voices growing louder each time. When they finished, their wings fluttered madly for several seconds—so fast that Rose could not see that they were wings at all. Then, in an instant, they all stopped and fell into the girls' laps, exhausted.

"Are they all right?" Snow asked, peering worriedly at the pair of fairies in her lap. She reached out and touched one very, very softly.

Rose bit her lip, unsure of the answer. She had never seen her fairies look like this before.

"We're fine," Dahlia explained in a voice so faint Rose had to strain to hear what she was saying. "It's just that trying to undo a spell takes every ounce of energy we have to give."

From beneath a gather in the skirt of Rapunzel's gown, Pansy opened an eye. "I think we may have done it," she said, sounding pleased but fatigued.

"But we cannot be sure until opening night," Viola warned. Rose could see that, tiny bit by tiny bit, the fairies were regaining their energy. Thank goodness.

"We should call off the play," Buttercup whispered fretfully. "Just to be safe."

Rose shook her head so hard Daisy almost fell off her lap. "No," she said flatly. "The show must go on."

Chapter Seventeen

Showtime

Rose paced back and forth onstage behind the lowered curtain. In less than half an hour, *The Tale of the Scary Fairy* would begin! Backstage, everyone was abuzz with activity. Ella and the costume crew were dressing the actors in their dramatic finery, while the make-up crew applied their stage makeup.

Already costumed and made up, Rose peeked around the heavy red curtain at the bustling auditorium and felt her heart beating in her chest. The hall was crowded with people! Many of the lush velvet seats were already filled, and large bunches of royals chatted regally in the aisles. Queens and ladies wore fancy gowns trimmed in lace, jewels, and ribbons. Kings and lords were in equal finery, with brocade vests and velvet breeches. Their crowns sparkled in the theater lights!

Rose spotted Kastrid and Ella's father, already seated in the middle of the house. Ella's father looked around somewhat timidly, but Kastrid looked smug, like she knew a secret. *She probably thinks Hag and Prune are the stars,* Rose thought. Rose's own parents sat in the second row, looking anxious. Her mother was wringing her hands, and her father kept getting to his feet, searching the auditorium, and sitting down again. And they didn't even know about Nettle's curse.

Rose felt a pang of guilt. Her parents had worked hard to protect her her entire life, and now she was putting herself in danger! *But the fairies broke the curse,* Rose told herself. She could only hope it had worked.

In the front row, Snow sat, wide-eyed, with Dap and Val, their friends from the nearby Charm School for Boys. Dap's legs were so long they practically stretched all the way to the stage. Val was dressed in his fanciest green tunic, and his black leather boots were polished to a shine. But Snow was the one who held Rose's gaze. Against the red velvet seat she was sitting in, she looked pale as milk!

Don't worry, Snow! Rose thought. Her own heart was beating fast, but not with fear—with exhilaration. It was opening night! Nothing was going to take this wonderful experience away from Rose and her friends—not even an angry little fairy and his curse.

"Places!" Calliope called in a whisper. Rose could see the excitement in the director's eyes as well. It was showtime!

Rose took her place stage left. Above and slightly behind her, Nettle hovered in the air. Rose shivered, suddenly feeling vulnerable. She was glad that for most of the play she would face Nettle and not have her back to him.

As the lights in the auditorium went down, a hush fell over the audience. The music began to play. Finally, the curtain rose. Rose held her breath—this was the moment of truth.

"Today you shall hear *The Tale of the Scary Fairy*," the narrator said clearly. "A tale of evil, woe, and triumph. For once upon a time there lived a dashing prince called Gallant and a lovely princess called Perfecta."

That was her cue. Rose strolled elegantly to center stage, while Rapunzel crossed from the other side to meet her. But even from the other side of the stage Rose could tell something was very wrong. There was perspiration on Rapunzel's brow, and she was the color of a brussels sprout!

Perhaps she is just worried about the curse, Rose thought worriedly, knowing that that was unlikely. Rapunzel faced danger like others faced a mirror.

Painfully slowly, Rapunzel crossed to center stage. *Thank goodness,* Rose thought when she finally arrived. But when Rapunzel turned to the audience to recite her line, her face went green. With horror, Rose realized Rapunzel was about to throw up!

Rose quickly pulled her shawl off her shoulders. There was not much she could do, but she could at least spare her friend the humiliation of losing her lunch in front of the enormous crowd. Then, out of the corner of her eye, she saw Ella springing into action backstage. Within seconds, Ella stood next to Rose wearing a brightly colored ruffled shirt, pantaloons, and heavy boots. Swiping the crown from Rapunzel's head, she gave her nauseous friend a tiny shove toward the side curtain.

Holding her hand over her mouth, Rapunzel managed a queasy but grateful look in Ella's direction as she hurried offstage.

Crisis averted! Rose thought as Ella squared her shoulders in a princelike manner. But the audience wasn't so sure. Alarmed whispers echoed in the hall as the theatergoers stared confusedly at the stage.

"Music!" Rose heard Calliope call quietly. "Replay the prelude!"

The musicians quickly turned back to the first page of their scores and began to play again. Then the narrator reread the introduction and Ella began to speak.

"I am a gallant prince in search of a fair maiden who might love me and become my bride," she said, bowing deeply. "Alas, it has been a long search."

Rose grinned. Ella was a natural! And she seemed thrilled to be onstage instead of behind the scenes.

109

Rose took a deep breath. The show was finally on the road.

"I am Princess Perfecta, a coddled young lady who longs for adventure and the love of a young prince. Alas, it has been a long wait...."

Chapter Eighteen
Showdown

Rose had not even finished her first line when she realized that something was amiss. The energy in the auditorium seemed to be...lagging. Lowering her gaze slightly, she eyed the royals sitting in the velvet seats and gasped. The audience was asleep!

Snores—quiet and not so quiet—filled the auditorium. Rose looked to her friends in the front row for support, but even they were dozing!

Rose's mind reeled. Obviously the curse had been softened but not broken. Nettle's spell had worked in reverse. She herself was wide awake. But the audience was totally out!

Panic filled every inch of Rose's body. This was terrible! They had to do something! She turned to Ella just in time to see her prince fall to the floor with a very unprincely thud, landing next to Hem and Haw. The rest of the cast was out cold as well!

Rose stood alone onstage amid a very heavy silence. And then she heard a frighteningly familiar voice in the wings. "What? No swoon? No cheer? No clap? You've forced your fans to take a nap!"

Nettle swooped to center stage, hovering at Rose's eye level. He cackled. Then, in a flash, he dropped his hood and removed his tiny protective gloves, letting them fall to the floor.

Rose eyed the fairy, completely unafraid. He was challenging her, and Rose was up to the challenge!

One finger at a time, Rose removed her own lace gloves. Fury welled within her. "How can you ruin the play after we've all worked so hard?!" she shouted.

"How could *I* ruin everything? It's *you* who ruined me!" Nettle shot back. "I lost everything when you were born! Your parents...they...I can't help that I sting!" Suddenly Nettle sounded more miserable than mad.

Rose felt confused. Was Nettle upset because Queen Comely and King DoGood—Princess Perfecta's parents—had wronged his character, the Scary Fairy? "Nettle, it's only a play," Rose said calmly.

Nettle looked thoroughly put out. "Hmmmph," he grumbled. "That's what you think."

Rose was wondering what the fairy was talking about when Rapunzel suddenly rushed in from back-stage, followed by a fleet of frantic fairies.

112

"Don't look at her!" Petunia warned, crashing into Dahlia.

"You'll fall into a terrible slumber!" Buttercup added, nearly colliding with Viola.

The flying swarm was so intent on not looking at Rose that they didn't look where they were going either. When they finally reached Nettle, they were a swarming tangle of color. And Rapunzel looked quite like her usual self as she stared hard at Nettle with her arms crossed over her tunic.

Rose stepped closer to gauge the look on Nettle's face. He truly seemed unhappy.

"Careful, Rose!" Pansy called out.

"Don't touch him!" Viola shouted in her tiny voice. "It will sting!"

Rose shooed them away and stepped even closer. "Look, Nettle," Rose said sincerely, "even if my parents did insult you, how can you hold that against me? I had nothing to do with it! And all those other royals who are under your sleeping spell—they *really* had nothing to do with it."

Nettle's tiny face contorted into a scowl and he crossed his arms across his chest. But he said nothing.

"My parents are always protecting me," Rose went on. "That seems to be the thing they work hardest at, and believe me, it is a thorn in my side." She sighed, wishing her parents could be more normal. But she supposed they were doing the best they could.

"Now..." Rose reached out and took the fairy's tiny hand. Her finger stung where it touched him. "Can we get on with the show? I do so admire and enjoy your acting. It's...it's like a gift. One I have been meaning to thank you for, for a long time." Then, without thinking, Rose leaned in and kissed Nettle lightly on the forehead. "So, thank you."

"Rose!" Tulip cried.

"Your ruby lips!" Daisy moaned.

Rose's lips stung like fire the moment they touched Nettle's skin, but she paid no attention. She was too focused on the little fairy. For the first time since Rose had met him he looked peaceful. A tiny purple tear slid down his pale green cheek.

Then, as suddenly as they'd slumbered, the audience and cast began to stir. They awoke with big stretches and yawns. Ella got to her feet, raised her arms over her head, and blinked.

"This show is over," Rapunzel told Rose's fairies, quickly shooing them offstage. "It's time for the play to begin."

Stage right, the narrator straightened her scarlet cape, picked her story book up off the floor, and began to read:

"And they all lived happily...Ooops!" Realizing

she'd lost her place, she quickly flipped back to the beginning.

"Once upon a time…"

"…and they all lived happily ever after."

The curtain lowered, and the audience clapped wildly. "Bravo!" people shouted. "Encore!" Rose could see Rapunzel in the wings, clapping and whistling.

By the time the curtain was raised again so that the cast could take a bow, the audience was on its feet. Rose could see her parents beaming in the second row. Ella's father was cheering loudly in the middle of the house, bursting with pride for his daughter, next to a grumbling Kastrid. Snow's face was rosy as she jumped up and down with glee. Val threw a giant bouquet of roses to Princess Perfecta, which Rose handed out to all the cast members. The last one she handed to Nettle.

"Careful of the thorns," she said with a wink.

Then the cast took a final bow, and the curtain closed for the last time.

About the Authors

Jane B. Mason grew up in Duluth, Minnesota, where a round stone tower graces the top of the city's hillside. (Fortunately, she was never trapped inside.) She had a strict mother and three older sisters who made her do her share of chores but never tried to keep her home from a school dance.

Sarah Hines Stephens grew up in Twain Harte, California, where she caught frogs in the woods but rarely kissed them. She can't talk to birds and she is hardly royalty, but her name does mean "princess," and after dating a toad or two she married a real prince of a guy.

Currently, Sarah and Jane lead charmed lives in Oakland, California. They are great friends and love to write together. Some of their other books include *The Little Mermaid and Other Stories, Heidi, Paul Bunyan and Other Tall Tales, The Legend of Sleepy Hollow, The Nutcracker, The Jungle Book,* and *King Arthur,* all Scholastic Junior Classics, and *The Best Christmas.* Between them, Sarah and Jane have two husbands, five kids, three dogs, one cat, and a tomato worm named Bob.

Ella's evil steps are in town— and they're stepping all over her!

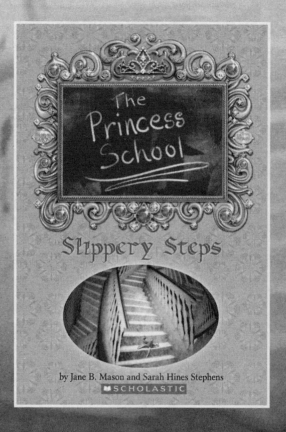

It's bad enough that Ella has to live with her mean stepmother and stepsisters. But now, the stepmother's evil stepfamily is coming to visit! Soon Ella is caught in the middle of a nasty family feud where she really has to watch her every step!

www.scholastic.com/princessschool

■SCHOLASTIC

PS8T

Go to school with Ella, Snow, Rapunzel, and Rose.

They're four friends who wait for no prince, but they're waiting for YOU at their own special Web site. You don't need a golden coach or a fairy godmother—just a click of the mouse takes you there.

scholastic.com/princessschool

Mirror, mirror on the wall, which book is the funniest of them all?

$4.99 Each

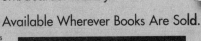